A Glowing Treasure

A GLOWING TREASURE

Elsie W. Strother

AVALON BOOKS
THOMAS BOUREGY AND COMPANY, INC.
NEW YORK

PRINTED IN THE UNITED STATES OF AMERICA
BY HADDON CRAFTSMEN, SCRANTON, PENNSYLVANIA

A Glowing Treasure

Chapter One

Alexis Steele opened the flattish, square package with misgivings. Her brother, Frank, had sent some nice prints and a few attractive original paintings to her gallery in the past, but lately, among his offerings, there had been some work of exceptional hideousness.

The very last painting had stunned her. It was a rendition of a poodle done in an aggressive bubble-gum pink. The paint was put on so thickly it resembled a huge wad of bubble gum, too. How could his taste have slipped so?

1

When Frank had first been sent to Asia, he'd sent lovely washy prints of rainy landscapes. The pink poodle was the worst of his offerings. There had also been a very gaudy painting of an Oriental temple and an unappealing abstract in violent purple and green.

Alexis's heart was bumping uncomfortably against her ribs with the suspense of the moment as she pulled off the last of the padded wrapping. When the picture was revealed, she at first looked stunned, then stared gloomily at the dreadful thing. How could he? What had happened to Frank's artistic discernment? This acrylic painting was of a cat, and there was junk glued to it: two huge opalescent plastic eyes and some big, cheap-looking glass beads that were around the cat's neck. How could her very own brother do this to her?

The painting was simply awful. It was the pits! There wasn't one solitary thing to redeem the mess. It would join the pink poodle and the abstract and the Oriental temple in the back-room closet.

Lexi, as her friends called her, lived in

a small, comfortable apartment above the Steele Gallery. Asheville had been her home before her mother and father had been killed in an auto accident and before Frank had joined an import-export firm in New York.

She'd seen this funny house—with its big lower story and much smaller second story—when driving through the countryside with friends and quickly arranged to buy it. She made the ground floor into a gallery and the second story into a little apartment for herself. It was a dear place.

Lexi had always loved the resort town of Lookaway Mountain in North Carolina. It should be a good place for an art gallery, she had thought, with its big inn and many private rustic summer cottages, as well as those owned by the inn. It attracted families that returned year after year. A golf course, tennis courts, and a lake for swimming and fishing brought plenty of vacationers. And the season began very early, in March. During the cooler months of the year, when few tourists appeared in Lookaway Mountain, Lexi supplemented her income with her handicraft work: knitting, crocheting, embroidery, and so forth. She made sweaters, tablecloths, and all kinds of lovely things that she sold to boutiques in the big cities.

Lexi's gallery was just outside the inn's grounds. Near her was a post office, a general store, a drugstore, several small frame houses, and the headquarters of the volunteer fire department. All were within walking distance of the inn and its cottages.

The bell on the door made its tinkling ring as Lexi was putting the dreadful cat picture out of sight in the small back room she used as a workshop and as storage space.

A very handsome young man entered the gallery and started walking around. His eyes quickly scanned the various paintings, resting for a moment on a small sculpture of a panther. Then he turned to Lexi, who had seated herself behind the desk near the front.

"I'm looking for a painting of a dog," he said. "It's going to be a joke on a friend, so I don't want anything really good. I'd prefer something awful—the junkier, the better."

"I'm afraid I don't sell junky paintings," Lexi said, "and the only thing I have with a dog is that hunting scene near the door. Its price is eighteen hundred."

"That's much too attractive and much too expensive," the young man said. "Don't you have something really dreadful, amateurish, garish? This is for a joke. I want something terrible!"

Lexi's mind flew to the bubble-gum poodle in the back room, but nothing that crude would ever be sold in her gallery.

"No, I'm sorry," she said. "I can't help you. All I can suggest is for you to drive to Asheville or someplace. I try very hard to handle only the best art available—within my relatively modest price range—so I hope you'll never find something really awful here."

"I see. Well, that's too bad. By the way, my name is Jeff Warner." The young man smiled as he leaned across the desk and looked deep into Lexi's warm brown eyes.

"You're very pretty."

"Thank you." Lexi felt uncomfortable. "As I said, you might have to go to Asheville to find what you want." She wished he'd stop staring at her.

"Your hair is the color of golden honey, isn't it? But your eyes and lashes are almost black. It's a lovely combination."

"Well, thank you again." Lexi stood up. "I'm sorry I can't help you, and now I must return to my workshop."

"Will you have dinner with me tonight? At the inn or any place you prefer."

"No, I won't. I mean, I can't. I—I'm going to be busy. And now please—"

"I don't want to go away. I'm going to look around the walls some more. I see you have some nice Japanese and Chinese watercolors. Do they come from the Orient? Or were they painted in the States?"

"From the Orient. My brother sent them to me."

"Does he send you other things, too?"

"Like what?"

"Oh, I don't know. Silly things, maybe."

Lexi was becoming perturbed. The way

this man was talking made her think he might know about the dreadful pictures her brother had been sending recently. He was too inquisitive.

It seemed almost a deliverance to Lexi when the doorbell rang again and another young man entered. He was quite different in appearance from the first one.

Where Jeff Warner was blue-eyed and blond, this new customer had black hair and cold gray eyes. Both men were tall and muscular.

As the newcomer started walking slowly around the gallery, Jeff headed for the door.

"I'll be back, beautiful," he said. "And if you get what I'm in the market for, save it, won't you?"

"Yes, I will, but there's little hope that—"

"Never give up hope, darling. See you."

Lexi was glad to see Jeff Warner leave. She turned to look at the other man and found him staring at her. What was the matter with everybody? Or was something wrong with her? Did she have paint on her nose? Was her dress torn, or was she wearing unmatched earrings? There must be something odd in her appearance.

"May I help you?" she asked in a rather small voice.

The man's gray eyes were so clear and sharp they seemed to penetrate her.

"I'm looking for imported works of art," he answered in a very deep and rather soothing voice. "I really want something Oriental. But not the usual Oriental stuff and nothing like those," he added, pointing to two Japanese reproductions. "I'm looking for something that's a bit different. I can't describe exactly what I want, but I'll know it when I see it."

"You're the second person within the hour to ask for something I haven't got. First a tacky painting of a dog and now an imported work that's not the usual. But you can't describe it. This is not my day." A small, uncertain laugh escaped her.

Beneath the man's hostile gray eyes, a smile appeared like a bit of warmth, then quickly disappeared.

"The man who just left," he said softly,

"was he the one who wanted the tacky picture of a dog?"

"Yes," she answered a little helplessly.

"Is this all you have?" He made a sweeping gesture of the walls.

"I have a few unframed paintings and two or three unpriced sculptures in my storage room, but nothing you'd be interested in, I'm sure."

"May I take a look?" he asked.

"Well, no, I'm sorry. You'll have to take my word for it. The storage room and my apartment upstairs are—are private."

"Sorry. May I come back again? You might have what I need later. My name is Keith Hamilton and I'm with the—no, never mind. I'll return soon. Goodby."

She was turning to go to the back room when he popped in the front door again.

"Miss." There was stark urgency in his voice. "If you live upstairs, are you quite safe, do you think? Do you have dead bolts on your doors? And is this gallery secure?"

"This is a very safe place, sir," Lexi answered. "We have only respectable people in the area, and the inn's vacationers are nice family people. I *do* lock the gallery, but my apartment—"

"So you don't have dead bolts. I suggest you get them for both your apartment and the gallery, and get them today! Please!"

He left her in a state of alarm. Lexi had never been fearful of living here alone, never. But this nosy stranger had put quivering little doubts into her mind.

The doorbell rang again and a middle-aged man and woman walked in together.

"May we browse?" the woman asked.

"Please do," Lexi said. She was pleased to have her fearful thoughts interrupted and dispelled.

The man was a pale little creature, and he wore glasses that looked as thick as ice cubes. His wife—if that was what she was—wore very heavy makeup and spoke in a loud, dramatic way. Neither of them, Lexi thought, looked at all typical of this resort area.

"I like that one," the man said, pointing to a watercolor by Carroll Rivers.

"Yes, Rivers is one of our very best local artists," Lexi said.

She was going to say more when the woman frowned at the painting. "I don't like it. Come on, let's go."

"I like it," the man insisted. "It's pretty."

But the woman had already rushed out of the door and the little man followed, sending one last yearning look at the Rivers work.

Lexi thought of the tall, dark, gray-eyed man. He was awfully attractive and perhaps he was right about locks. All sorts of people were likely to pass through a resort town like Lookaway Mountain. Maybe she'd be wise to follow the advice of—what was his name? Keith something.

She closed the gallery. It was almost closing time, anyway, and if she hurried, she'd get to the general store before it shut its doors. Lexi ran the short distance as fast as she could.

"Mr. Harris," she said, panting a little from the exertion, "have you got a dead bolt?"

"Dead bolts in Lookaway? Why, honey, dead bolts are for high-risk areas, cities and such. Why would you—"

"What kind of locks do you have then?"

"Well, I got a couple plain bolts some-where in the back, I think. You'd have to go to Asheville if you want dead bolts. Want I should find the plain bolts for you?"

"Please. Just one will do. For my apart-ment, you know."

"Okay. And while you wait, look over them new plums I got in. Pure delicious, they are."

Lexi picked out a half dozen plums, a dozen eggs, a can of hair spray, and a tube of toothpaste before Mr. Harris came back.

"Found it," he said. "And you'll need screws to put it up with. Want a screw-driver?"

Alexis paid for everything and hurried back. She'd never before worried about being safe. It was unnerving. Darn that gray-eyed man! She climbed up the out-side stairs to the apartment and got to work on that door.

Then she began to have second thoughts about the whole thing. It seemed silly, positively absurd, to make her simple apartment burglar-proof. What was there to steal?

But for some strange reason Lexi felt pleasantly relieved when all was locked up. She remembered the handsome man, Jeff, who wanted a painting of a dog, who complimented her extravagantly, and who said he'd be back. Was she locking him out? He was brash, and she couldn't stand brash people.

She looked around her little three-room apartment. The small bedroom was fairly attractive and so was the kitchen. But it was the living room that really filled her with pride. She had scandalized the house painters (Carolina mountain men with set notions) when she demanded dark-blue walls and white woodwork in the living room. The upholsterer had frowned quite a bit when she chose a pale blue-and-green print on a white background for her furniture (so easily soiled, so impractical).

When she bought a few white throw pillows and covered the floor with white carpeting, the local people considered her quite mad (not a thought for the spring mud). She partially quelled their belief in her insanity when she ordered pale-gray paint for the walls of the gallery (getting sensible at last, poor girl).

Lexi adored her apartment, small though it was. It looked just the way she wanted it to. Through the large picture window in the living room, she could see the mellowed surface of Stone Mountain some miles away, which seemed to complement the freshness of her color scheme. And in the evenings, with the long, heavy white drapes pulled, the coziness of her apartment was heavenly.

But now, as Lexi puttered in her cheerful yellow kitchen, a small, niggling worry kept gnawing at her. Her brother, Frank—why was he sending her those awful paintings? Was it a joke or could he possibly see some virtue in them? Could he have been conned into believing they represented a new wave in the art world and would be worth a lot someday? Whoever had convinced him—if that were the case—had the artistic appreciation of a bulldozer. The bubble-gum poodle and the plastic-eyed cat would reside in the locked closet in the back room with the first two monstrosities until Frank retuned to the States. Lexi hoped he'd have an explanation.

She had worked herself into a state of irritation now. Then she remembered that her last four letters to Frank had not been answered. That was very inconsiderate—altogether too casual—very, *terribly* unlike him! And now her irritation turned into apprehension.

Frank was her beloved brother, her only close relative, and it distressed her not to know how he was, how his business trip was coming along. The only communications she'd had lately were the dreadful paintings. And not a word from him had accompanied the packages.

Lexi's bedroom was carpeted in beige, and the walls were a pale-blue. They were covered with her own artwork: some acrylics, some pastels, and quite a few watercolors. She wasn't yet good enough, she felt, to be hung in the gallery downstairs, but the color and variety of subject matter gave the room a touch of liveliness.

After a simple supper and an hour or two spent in studying the history of art,

Lexi usually indulged herself by reading a light novel before going to bed. She did so tonight.

A full moon shone in her bedroom window. Full moons somehow made her restless, unable to enjoy her usual deep sleep, and perhaps it was the moon that kept her edgy this night.

The house was old, and its creaking and moaning and sudden rasps no longer bothered her. But tonight there were strange creeping sounds, hushed rustlings, and a sort of deep-breathing noise.

Lexi jumped out of bed and made a quick inspection of her apartment. There was nothing to be alarmed about. If some intruder were surveying her house, he was somewhere outside. She looked out her kitchen window in time to see a large cat skulking near the bushes. The moon shone into the creature's cold citrine eyes.

Lexi sighed with relief and returned to bed.

Chapter Two

Lexi was up early. Her night had not been restful and she was glad to start a new day. Remembering yesterday's nervousness, she looked out of her windows, all of them, and peered out her door at the late-summer day. Robins were pulling at their wormy breakfasts, the newsboy went whistling along, throwing his rolled-up papers, and some guests from the inn were taking a morning walk.

It was as peaceful as ever, and she berated herself for last night's imaginings. Her foolish fears were caused by the gray-eyed man and his warning. It wasn't like her to get all nervous for nothing.

At nine o'clock Lexi opened the gallery. There was unfinished work in the back room—two mats to cut, a frame to paint, and the closet to tidy up. The poodle, the cat, the temple, and the abstract must be covered and put into the far recesses of the closet. She wanted to throw them out, but, of course, she couldn't do that. She'd discuss them with Frank and then return them to the artist, if you could call them artists.

She was finishing with the frame when the doorbell rang.

"Oh, shucks," she growled under her breath. "Nobody buys paintings this early in the morning! Oh, darn, and now my fingers are all messy!"

The bell rang again and Lexi ran from the back room calling, "All right! I'm coming! I'm coming!"

Already inside the gallery, Jeff Warner, a wide grin on his handsome face, said, "I told you I'd be back!"

"Oh, it's you! What do you..."

"What do I want? Well, sweetie, I'll tell

you. I want a terrible painting of a dog and—I know, I know! You haven't got one. And I want to take you to dinner tonight."

Lexi was annoyed at the man's persistence. She really didn't feel comfortable with him. He was too handsome, too pushy, and he gave her a nervous feeling.

She made her big brown eyes as vacant as possible and looked at him, she hoped, with idiocy. She didn't know what to say, but surely he'd change his mind about dating a dummy.

Instead, his smiling face took on the predatory look of a crocodile. She felt a twinge of alarm.

"Thank you," she said quickly, letting her normal intelligence flow back into her pretty face. "I must tell you again that I *haven't* got the dog picture you want, and I can't and won't go to dinner with you! Thanks again and now I must get back to my work, so—"

"You mean I'm to go away? Is that the way to treat a prospective customer? A customer who's entranced by your honey-gold hair and your dirty hands?"

Lexi had to smile then. He had a sense

of the ridiculous. Perhaps he wasn't as forward or as brazen as she'd thought.

"That's what I mean," she said, but her expression was more cordial now. "I *do* have work to do, you know. So please go."

At that moment the door was pushed open, making the bell ring, and a woman in handsome, citified clothes came in. Her topaz eyes took in the walls, the paintings, Alexis, and Jeff in one sweeping glance.

"I'm Rosalyn Gray," she said and looked expectant, as if her name should mean something to someone.

"Good morning," Lexi said.

"I have a letter for you," the woman said.

Jeff beamed at both young women. "One of my most endearing characteristics is that I know when I'm not wanted. I'll see you later, darling." And he strode out of the gallery.

"A—a letter for me?" Lexi said with surprise.

"Yes. It's from your brother. I'll just look around while you read it."

Lexi took the letter with an eager hand. Word from Frank at last! But why didn't he send it through the mails? Was he back in the States? She sat at her desk and tore open the envelope.

"Dear Alexis..." The typed words looked strange. Frank never called her Alexis unless he was angry at her, and that hadn't happened in a long time.

She continued to read. "The bearer of this letter is Rosalyn Gray, my fiancée. I'm sure you will soon become as devoted to her as I am. Now, Alexis dear, Rosalyn has nowhere to live until I come home, and I told her that she could room with you and help in the gallery. She's very knowledgeable about art. You'll do this for me, won't you? Much love from your big brother."

It was signed "Frankie."

Lexi stared at the short letter. Why had he called her Alexis? Why had he signed the letter with the name "Frankie" when he always used a simple "Frank"? Why did the signature look a little odd? Why was he asking her to house this stranger when he knew darn well her small apartment was designed for one person? And how could he think she needed an assistant at the gallery? Above all, why had he never told her he was engaged or even that he'd met someone important to him?

It was so confusing and not very pleasant. In fact, it was almost frightening because it didn't sound like Frank at all. But then, maybe he'd changed since he'd gotten engaged. People did change.

"You have read it?" The young woman faced Lexi with a rather low-wattage smile. "Frank has told me so much about you. How very generous you are, how warm and kind. I know we'll be dear friends."

Lexi looked questioningly at the woman. "You and Frank are engaged? But he never told me—"

"We met in Japan and it was love at first sight. I'm sure he meant to write you about us, but you know how young lovers are."

"No. How are they?" Lexi's stomach had shrunk to the size of a peanut. What in the name of Allah, Buddha, Thor, or Jupiter, as Frank liked to say, was she going to do? Being angry with her brother, so far away, was like fighting with fog.

Rosalyn's laugh tinkled like the doorbell. "He forgot to tell me you had a sense of humor."

"My sense of humor is lacking at the moment, I'm afraid. Frank had no right to tell you I could, or would, put you up or use you in the gallery. You can see the size of the gallery. And my apartment upstairs is even smaller. It's a one-woman place. I'm really very sorry to be so inhospitable, but—"

"Oh, my dear sister-in-law-to-be, I'm not fussy. I can sleep on a couch or a cot in that messy place back there." She pointed to the open door of the back room.

"I couldn't have you do that. No, if you plan to stay around Lookaway Mountain, I'm sure I can arrange an accommodation at the inn. It's nice there. Uh, how soon do you expect my brother? He hasn't written me his plans."

"No exact date. He wants me to get to

know you well and he said you'd soon love me as he does." Rosalyn's voice was throaty with smugness.

Lexi felt a surge of distaste for this girl who had won Frank's admiration and love. Maybe it was not so much distaste as an aching indifference. Rosalyn Gray was the kind of female Lexi had always avoided. She had thought that Frank's taste was like hers, but how wrong she'd been! Now it was important that she begin to look for the young woman's good qualities. She wouldn't hurt her brother for the world, and if he wanted her to like his fiancée, then, by golly, she'd try to.

"Let me wash up a bit, Rosalyn, and I'll take you to the inn. Bob Pierce, the manager, is a good friend."

"May I wash, too?" Rosalyn asked.

"Oh, of course. You—you'll have to come upstairs with me. I only have an old sink in the back room."

"That's all right. I'll wash in the sink."

"No, come along. I'll lock the gallery and we'll go up."

"What a charming place!" Rosalyn exclaimed when they had entered the apartment.

Lexi liked her better for that.

But then Rosalyn said, "Why couldn't I sleep on the sofa? It looks comfy."

"It is." How could she tell Rosalyn that she didn't want, and wouldn't allow, an intruder in her cherished private home? "But not for spending nights on. You'll be comfortable at the inn. Here's the bathroom. There are clean towels over the basin."

It was a walk of only five minutes from the gallery to the inn, but Rosalyn's stiletto heels slowed them down.

Bob Pierce was delighted to see Lexi and seemed rather smitten with Rosalyn. Lexi thought that fact interesting. To her, Rosalyn wasn't very attractive, but now she tried to look at her with both Frank's and Bob's eyes. Rosalyn was smartly dressed, of course. Her black silk suit and ruffled white blouse were well-made. Her hair was sleekly wound into a chignon and its color was a lovely auburn. No doubt touched up, Lexi thought cattily.

Rosalyn's topaz eyes were quite spectacular and she batted her mascara at the manager for all she was worth.

"Of course, we'll find a room for her, Lexi," he said. "Any friend of yours—"

"Thank you, Bob. Oh, Rosalyn, I forgot to ask you about your bags. Where are they? At the store near the bus stop?"

Bob said, "I'll see to her bags, Lexi. Don't you worry."

"I'll be going back to my gallery then," Lexi said. "Goodby."

"Oh, Lexi!" Bob stopped her. "Why don't you and our lovely newcomer have dinner here with me tonight?"

"Sorry, Bob—" Lexi began.

"Oh, do accept, Alexis," Rosalyn said. "You and I must get to know one another, and this sweet man here will help us."

Lexi had a twinge of annoyance. Bob, who was a widower, had squired her around a bit, escorting her to barn dances and hayrides. She'd never been greatly attracted to him, but to watch him almost melt at Rosalyn's feet was provoking. Her vexation made up her mind. Lexi would accept and wear her most becoming outfit and she'd show this—this witch she was not to be put in the shade. Or on the shelf or whatever.

Then Lexi had a moment of shame. This young woman was adored by her brother and she must be kind to her and control her own vicious instincts. After all, by being good to Rosalyn, she was protecting Frank's interests, wasn't she?

On her way back to the gallery, Lexi made herself take a good look at her mean impulses. Why did she resent Rosalyn? Was it because Frank had chosen her without a word to his sister? In a way, yes! And was it because the woman had forced her way into Lexi's life? Yes! And was it because Rosalyn could attract male attention with one arch look of her topaz eyes? Yes! Was all this just cause for her to dislike Rosalyn? If Lexi was that small-minded, yes!

In that case, she had better shape up. Frank wouldn't appreciate her aversion to Rosalyn. Lexi mentally shook herself and vowed to be extra pleasant to Frank's fiancée from now on. But she wouldn't often allow Rosalyn into her apartment and would frown on more than infrequent visits to the gallery. They could be friends with a substantial distance between them.

That evening Lexi changed into a coral linen dress, chunky white beads and earrings, and white sandals. As she put on a light jacket, she knew she looked her best and wondered what kind of glamorous outfit Rosalyn would wear.

A million or more frogs were all yelling "gronk" from the edges of the lake as Lexi walked to the inn. Soft clouds covered the sky with broken patterns of silver and dark-gray and cast vague shadows over the road. It was a lovely evening and Lexi's mood softened and mellowed in the rosy sunset. She was going to be nice. She was going to like her future sister-in-law, and she was going to enjoy the evening.

Bob was waiting for Lexi by the front desk and in a few minutes Rosalyn joined them. Rosalyn's dress was a pale-cream silk and complemented her lovely hair. Around her neck in a loose knot was a scarf, beige and gold, with touches of topaz to match her eyes. She was so chic she made other women look dowdy. Her gold jewelry was expensive without being ostentatious.

If Rosalyn could wear costly designer clothes and real jewelry, why had Frank said she needed a place to stay, as if she couldn't afford the inn? It was puzzling, but Lexi wasn't going to try to solve the puzzle tonight. She smiled at Rosalyn and made pleasant chitchat as Bob took their arms and led them to the dining room.

There were a hundred or more diners at tables that sat two, four, six, and eight people. Bob chose a table for four and didn't look displeased when Jeff Warner approached. Bob invited him to sit with them, thinking perhaps that Jeff would absorb Lexi's attention while he endeared himself to Rosalyn.

At least that was Lexi's annoyed opinion. Here she was, saddled with the obnoxious Jeff again, but she would try to be gracious. He had, after all, a sort of lazy grace, an elegance, a polished look.

It was obvious that Jeff and Rosalyn knew each other, Lexi noticed. Then she remembered he had been at the gallery when Rosalyn came in. Anyway, Jeff seemed uninterested in the glamorous girl and, despite Lexi's antipathy to Jeff, she was pleased at his lack of interest in the other young woman.

"So, my beauty," Jeff said, pretending to curl a wicked mustache like a melodrama villain, "you are having dinner with me, after all! You mustn't ask me if my intentions are honorable. I tend to lose my famed sweet temper when my intentions are questioned."

It was no use being offended by this blockhead, Lexi thought. It was hard to resist his idiocy, and she found herself laughing often during the meal.

When cherry cobbler and coffee were being enjoyed by everyone at the end of a delicious dinner, Lexi was pondering ways of putting off Jeff's probable offer to walk her home. Suddenly, a large shadow fell over her. She looked up.

"Good evening." It was the gray-eyed man, Keith Hamilton. "Please excuse my barging in on your dinner, but I wanted to make an appointment with you, Miss Steele. Will you name a time I can see you tomorrow?"

This was Lexi's out. She smiled. "Why not walk me back to the gallery tonight? We can discuss your business on the way. That's if you—"

"A fine idea," Keith said. "I'll wait for you on the veranda."

Jeff stood up. "Don't you know it's rude to break in on a date, Hamilton? Miss Steele and I were having dinner together, as you can see."

Lexi saw Keith's eyes turn bleak as winter. "I didn't have a date with you, Jeff," she said. "And now I have a business appointment with Mr. Hamilton. Bob, it was a lovely dinner and thank you. Rosalyn, sleep well."

"I'll see you tomorrow," Rosalyn said.

Lexi shook her head. "I'm going to be busy tomorrow. Why don't you get into a golf game or swim or something."

"Yes," Bob said happily, "let's play a round of golf, Rosalyn, or would you rather play tennis?"

Lexi left them chatting pleasantly.

Jeff was beside her as she stepped out to the wide veranda. "I'll come, too," he said.

"No, you won't." Keith had risen from a bench. His eyes were a hard ice-gray peering through slitted lids.

Chapter Three

"I hope," said Keith, holding Lexi's elbow lightly as they walked from the inn to the road, "that I didn't interrupt a pleasant evening. I'm afraid I'm often abrupt and untactful."

"It's all right," Lexi said, gently disengaging her arm from his. "I was Bob Pierce's guest, not Jeff's." She took a deep breath. The sweet smells of freshly mowed grass, of moist earth, of pine trees flavored the air. "Isn't it delicious? If you've ever lived in a city, you know how wonderful all this is."

"Yes, I know. Alexis—is that what you're called, and may I call you that?"

"Only those who don't know me well call me Alexis. My friends call me Lexi."

"I want to be a friend, Lexi. Did you put dead bolts on your doors?"

"A bolt, but not the dead variety," Lexi chuckled softly. "Mr. Harris at the store thought I'd lost my marbles when I asked for a dead bolt. You see, this is not a crime-ridden area, Mr. Hamilton."

"Call me Keith. That young woman you were with at dinner, do you know her well?"

"No, not well at all. She arrived today and said she was my brother's fiancée and wanted to stay with me! Of all things!"

"You didn't agree to let her stay with you, did you?"

"Of course not. When you see my apartment, you'll know why a guest would be impossible."

All of a sudden, Lexi realized she'd said "when" not "if" and wondered at herself. She had a strange feeling that she sort of wanted Keith to see her place. She'd like his admiration—and she sensed he'd approve of her decorating—and it might be pleasant to know him better.

A spiteful, annoying little wind started up and Lexi wrapped her arms around herself.

"A change of weather, I think," Keith said. "You know, I believe that girl, your brother's intended, is transparently a money-minded ferret. I hope I'm not hurting you by saying that. She's the type I'd stay away from if I were you."

"How can I? My brother, Frank, asked me to put her up, to use her in the gallery, and he expects me to become fond of her. I—I'm *not* fond of her, not yet, but I hope I'll learn to appreciate her good qualities sooner or later."

They arrived at the gallery.

"My apartment is upstairs," Lexi said. "Would you like to have some coffee?"

"Good night, Lexi. I never did get around to talking business, so I'll be back to see you. Sleep well."

He faded into the black-and-silver night, which enfolded him as if he were a wisp of smoke, leaving Lexi frustrated. Very seldom did she invite anyone up to her apartment, and that such a privileged person should not accept was outrageous!

Suddenly, she felt unloved. It was silly of her, she knew. Keith was a stranger, possibly married with ten children, but he was so terribly fascinating, and she wished—no, she mustn't wish. She forced herself to remember his gray eyes, which were as cold as those of a halibut and made her feel unattractive.

Why should *she* feel unappealing? There was always Jeff, who kept trying so hard to ingratiate himself with her. But she didn't want Jeff. Did that mean she wanted Keith? Certainly not, she told herself. He was nice, he was pleasant, and he held himself aloof, which gave him an intriguing air. That was all.

Lexi unlocked her door just as the first fat drops of rain descended. It would be a nice night for sleep, with rain pattering on the roof. But although she felt achingly tired, she was far from ready to sleep. Her mind reviewed the things that kept worrying her: the dreadful paintings her brother had sent, Frank's silence except for his uncharacteristic letter about Rosalyn; Jeff's unexplained attachment to Lexi, if that was what it was; Keith— what about Keith?

She fought a trembling sensation as he filled her mind, she fought a feeling of sweetness and tension. What was the matter with her? Falling in love without encouragement from the loved one? Lexi was filled with self-disgust now. She blew her nose, felt better, and went to bed.

When she awoke early the next morning, it was still raining, and quite heavily. Lexi thought of Rosalyn and Bob's plans to play golf or tennis and hoped that Rosalyn wouldn't appear at the gallery because of the cancellation of those plans. This was going to be a slow day—rain kept people at the inn or in their summer homes—and she'd have time to finish several chores in the back room and to dust the gallery. Or maybe she'd work on her own painting.

Lexi was doing a landscape, better than most of her attempts, she thought. If it turned out well, she'd be bold and hang it where the public could see it. It was an audacious plan, but she'd hang it in an inconspicuous corner.

Her thoughts were happy as she fixed her breakfast and got dressed in a paint-smeared smock. Gone was her brooding about unrequited love, gone her worries about the horrid paintings—let Frank worry about returning them when he came—and gone the annoyance at Jeff's persistence and Rosalyn's presence. This was her day and Lexi planned to make the most of it.

Not long after she'd started working on a rain-heavy cloud in her landscape, the doorbell rang. It was Keith.

"I haven't got time to talk now," he said, "but do you play golf?"

Lexi nodded. What did golf have to do with anything?

"Do you ever take a day off?" he asked.

"Mondays," she answered. "Hardly anybody buys paintings on Mondays."

"Will you play with me on Monday, then? On the inn's course?"

"I'm not very good, you know. My handicap is twenty. What's yours?"

"Six. But don't let that worry you. Today is Friday and I have to go to Greensboro, but I'll be back late Sunday. Meet me on the first tee at nine-thirty, will you? I'll make the arrangements. You look— well, I had a golden retriever once whose coat was the color of your hair. His eyes were dark like yours, too. I loved that dog. Goodby."

Lexi stood looking at the closed door, spellbound. Keith was an astounding man, abrupt but not quite rude. He'd likened her to a well-loved dog, and for that she should be grateful? Maybe she should.

She put him out of her mind and proceeded to put the finishing touches on her painting. She was working with acrylics and so the paint dried almost immediately. Lexi looked at the picture, head on one side, and wondered if she really dared hang it with the work of talented artists.

She liked it. It had a dreamy, wispy look, with its threat of a gentle rain and its mossy foreground. As a matter of fact, it had quite an Oriental atmosphere. She thought of Keith's original request for an Oriental painting that was unusual.

Might this come close to meeting his demands?

Probably not. Now she must find a place for it to hang. Lexi tried a space beside a marvelous landscape by Robert Alton that was not for sale because it had belonged to her mother. No, that wouldn't do. She tried several other places and finally settled for a space below a wildflower watercolor by Carroll Rivers. The space Lexi was taking was quite obscure, and the Rivers would attract eyes whereas *hers* would fade into the background. But the colors of the two blended beautifully and did nothing to spoil the ambience of the gallery. She was gratified to have found a solution and happy to have her own painting hanging among the works of talented professionals.

Despite her chores in the back room and her cleaning of the gallery, time was passing like a snail with a broken leg. Monday morning at nine-thirty was a million years away and because it seemed so far in the distance she was bored with the present.

Lexi even welcomed the interruption of

Jeff, who came to ask if she had found that painting he wanted.

"You see, dear," he said, "the man I want it for has a house filled with antlers and stuffed trout. You can see what a badly painted dog would add to it, can't you? And the joke is that he probably wouldn't know it was bad. It could look to be created by a demented child and he'd believe it good if someone, namely me, told him it was."

"That would be a mean trick, Jeff, and I'm glad I haven't got a dog picture for you."

"You're noble, darling. I'm not. Incidentally, you seem to be about sixteen with your painty smock and hair that looks as if it had been dragged backward through a bush. How would you like to be sixteen again?"

She grimaced. "I had a horrid time at sixteen."

"So did I. How about dinner tonight?"

"No thank you, Jeff. I'm not feeling terribly well today."

"Hmm. You look so healthy, your pic-

ture should be on a cereal box. But I'm
not insensitive. I'll wait and ask you tomorrow. Or the next day. Or the next. I'm
not called Bulldog Jeffrey for nothing! See
ya." He left, striding into the rain.

He was amusing. Lexi was not sure why
she kept on refusing his invitation. Other
girls would jump at the chance to date
such a handsome and entertaining young
man. Though she'd never thought about
it before, perhaps she preferred a more
reserved approach. Maybe she felt the
swaggering bombast of Jeff compared un-
favorably with the respectful, deferential
attitude of Keith. Yes, she admitted, she
was old-fashioned in that way. Perhaps
that was it. Perhaps.

There were a few visitors to the gallery
on Saturday and Sunday. One painting of
a flight of geese was sold and a print of a
Mexican market was reserved with a down
payment. Pretty poor business, Lexi la-
mented but without many regrets. Sales
in a gallery went up and down—good days
and bad—and to worry was foolish.

Rosalyn appeared late on Sunday with
a mesmerized Bob Pierce in tow. The wind

was blowing fiercely when they arrived, but all the same, not a hair of Rosalyn's oversprayed coiffure was out of place.

"I've brought this dear man," Rosalyn gushed, "to buy a painting from you. I told him the inn's lounge needs prettying up. Look around, Bob."

Lexi had uncomfortable thoughts about her brother being two-timed by his fiancée, but she hoped she was wrong. Rosalyn couldn't help attracting men. It didn't mean she was untrue to Frank.

Bob picked a print of Stone Mountain. "This should do," he said.

"But, sweetie!" Rosalyn protested. "You need something more colorful. And you mustn't be chintzy. A print is cheap and a painting isn't, so you mustn't pick a print! Let me choose something, won't you?"

With unerring taste Rosalyn went directly to a large oil, colorful with fall tints, its center of attraction being a pair of horses.

"Don't you think this is better, Alexis?" she asked.

She certainly knew, Lexi admitted. That

particular painting would look marvelous in the inn's rustic lounge. Lexi nodded.

"It's fairly expensive," she said. "Compared to the other paintings here."

"Oh, Bob doesn't mind. Do you, dear? It's for the inn, after all," Rosalyn said.

Soon they departed. The painting was wrapped and in Bob's arms, and Lexi's till was nicely fattened. She closed the gallery with a feeling of accomplishment. Tomorrow was Monday!

Her sleep was deep and dreamless, and hours before her golf date she was dressed in sky-blue shorts and a navy top. She polished her clubs and fastened them on a pull-cart. She disdained caddies and electric carts. When she played golf, she walked. Even if her game was poor, she got exercise.

Lexi was the earliest arrival at the first tee. She had come early purposely. She needed practice. With no one around, she would play the first hole and then come back to the tee to wait for Keith.

The first hole was not too far away, and Lexi could easily make the green in two. The fairway was narrow, with deep woods on both the left and the right, so only a straight drive would keep the player out of trouble. A slice or a hook could mean disaster.

After a few practice swings, Lexi teed up her ball and hit it. It wasn't her best drive by any means and sailed less than the distance she usually got. Scolding herself, she walked and pulled her cart up to her ball. She was choosing a club for her next shot when another player's ball went whizzing past her left shoulder.

Stunned and indignant, she turned. But where had the ball come from? There was nobody on the first tee. She could get a glimpse of the ninth tee through the trees on the right and realized it could have come from there. But there was no one there, either.

Lexi was puzzled and angry that anyone could be so careless, but she told herself that she was playing the hole without signing up and that whoever shot the wild ball didn't know she was on the fairway.

She took a number two wood, hit solidly, and had the satisfaction of seeing her ball land on the edge of the green. That was better. She had started walking again when there was a sharp thwack on her golf bag. A ball, yellow in color, had struck it hard enough to split the canvas. The ball had been meant to hit her.

Lexi felt her first twinge of fear—real fear, not nervousness. She had played golf for several years and never found the course a place of terror. But now, knowing she was the target of someone or other, she felt herself cringe with fright.

Chapter Four

A person can only stay scared so long. The fright stops and you stop shaking. You're surprised you're not trembling anymore and wonder why you feel almost normal except for a cold rage.

Lexi's thoughts turned inward. The attempt to hurt her, perhaps even kill her, had been deliberate. She had no enemies. At least she knew of no one who hated her, yet there *was* someone. Someone who was hidden in the trees, someone who had to be a superb golf player to have hit so close to the target.

Leaving her ball on the green, Lexi hurried, zig-zagging back to the tee. A moving object was hard to hit.

She ran into the pro shop.

"Is there anybody playing right now, Andy?" she asked. "Or anybody practicing?"

"No, Lexi. It's kinda early. I got you down for nine-thirty with a Mr. Hamilton. There's one couple ahead of you, that's all."

"How—how many people play with yellow balls these days?"

"Why, it's kinda the style now, Lexi. Yellow or orange. You want one?"

"No. But, Andy, I was walking up the first fairway when a ball came close to hitting me. And then another ball, this yellow one, hit my bag. Who do you suppose did that?"

Andy looked shocked. "You don't think that it was done on purpose, do you? Nobody would do something that dangerous. Maybe some kid was looking for balls in the woods and he knocked that one onto the freeway by accident."

"Yes. Maybe. Well, if it was a caddie,

you tell him to be careful, won't you?" Lexi didn't want to pursue the subject further. She had her own ideas.

"Yeah, sure, Lexi. I'll chew him out if I find who was so unthinking."

Lexi stayed near the pro shop until she saw Keith walking toward her.

"Lovely morning, isn't it?" he said.

Her eyes slid over his muscled, bronzed arms.

"Heavenly," she answered. "Shall we start?"

Lexi collected her gear and shot first. Her drive put her halfway to the green.

"Good shot!" Keith said.

When he teed up his ball, and Lexi saw it was yellow, she felt a sinking in the pit of her stomach. Deeper than the need to know if he were the one, was a fear of knowing. Why would he try to hurt her or frighten her, or how had he become her enemy? It was a fear she must find courage to defeat.

When he had hit his ball nearly to the green and they started walking, she took the step she dreaded.

"You were out early, weren't you? You

were looking for balls in the woods, weren't you?"

"No, I came to the tee right after breakfast," Keith said. "Why do you ask?"

Her heart was beating slowly, heavily, and she wished the knotted fist in her gut would go away.

"Someone tried to hurt me, or at least to frighten me."

She told him about the whizzing balls, about the last one being yellow, and watched him as a look of doubt crept into his eyes for an instant.

"And you think it's possible *I* was the one because I play with a yellow golf ball?" Keith's voice was as cold as his gray eyes.

"I—I don't know what to think."

"Aren't you scared to play golf with me, with all the long, lonesome fairways and no one but me around?"

Lexi's eyes were suspiciously bright behind their long lashes and Keith stopped walking.

"Look, Lexi, look at me." He put a hand on her arm, drawing her to him. "You *can't,* you *mustn't* believe I could harm you in any way. I'm going to tell you something that might have to do with the danger you were in, but first..."

He dropped his clubs and put his arms around her. She went to him gladly, eagerly, but he held her lightly, kissed her forehead, and let her go.

"I'm here because I'm investigating a fraud that has to do with artworks. That's why I came to your gallery. We've traced the stolen pieces as far as Lookaway Mountain."

"But all the paintings that are hanging in the gallery are by people I know, or know of, Keith. Is it a fake you're looking for?"

"No, and it's not necessarily a painting. I won't tell you more, dear, because it's safer for you not to know. And, anyway, your gallery isn't under suspicion—not entirely. But what I have to point out is that there might be somebody who wishes to scare you away, to clear the field in order to collect the stolen goods. Do I make myself clear?"

"No."

"Well, I can't explain any further. Would you consider going away for a week or so, Lexi?"

"I would not," she said.

"Even though there may be someone who wants you out of the way?"

"Even so. This is my home, the only one I have, and nobody is going to—" Lexi swallowed a lump in her throat. She was tense, on edge, like a small boat carrying too much sail. She whiffed her next shot.

"We won't count that, Lexi," Keith said.

"Yes, we will," she growled. "I'll probably shoot a hundred and twenty-four today. Shall we stop playing? This is no fun for you."

"Not unless *you* want to stop, Lexi. I enjoy being with you, and if you shoot three hundred, I'll still enjoy the day."

"All right, we'll keep on." She felt anger seething within her, rising to a boiling point that made her want to choke whoever had spoiled her day, whoever had tried to hurt her and was a continuing threat.

They finished nine holes and decided

against tackling the other nine. Keith had shot two over par and Lexi had refused to count her strokes, her game was so erratic.

"I don't usually play this badly," she apologized.

"Of course, you don't. I can't blame you for your lack of concentration. Now, Lexi, we've got the rest of the morning. What would you like to do? Swim? Play tennis? Hike?"

"Hike, I guess."

Overhead the sun burned through the blue-white of an overheated sky. The air hummed with insect sounds.

"It's not too hot for you?" Keith asked.

"We can walk in the woods. I—I want to explore the woods beside the first fairway, Keith. I want to look for a clue as to who my enemy is."

"Now, Lexi, it's not an enemy! It could have been an accident. Or maybe it's just someone who would like you to be absent. I'm sure that's it."

"I'm glad you're sure," she snapped. *"I'm not!"*

They left their clubs in the pro shop and walked toward the woods on the left side of the fairway. They were quiet, and the silence was strained.

Then, "I'm sorry," Lexi said. "I shouldn't bark at you. It's just that—" She stopped and fought back some threatening tears.

"I know," Keith said softly. "You've had a horrid morning, haven't you? Well, let's play detective in the woods. What are we looking for?"

"Clues."

"All right. Any lurking clues better be careful of our eagle eyes. We'll be intrepid in ferreting out every clue in the forest. Come, dear, cheer up!"

Lexi knew he was trying to reassure her, to encourage and comfort her. Her natural ebullience came to her rescue and she laughed uncertainly.

"Okay, I'll stop feeling sorry for myself. But I assure you that if I find out who ruined my whole day, I'll—I'll—"

"Hell will have no fury like your justified wrath. Good for you!"

It was steamy among the pine trees,

even before noon, and soon they were mopping their faces and necks.

They found several golf balls that had been all but hidden by brush or fallen limbs and left for lost. They found an empty beer can, one golf glove, and a small pile of tees. Nothing could be termed a clue, and soon they gave up the idea of a hike in the woods. It had become too sultry.

Lexi wanted a cool bath and refused Keith's invitation to lunch. She discouraged his offer to walk her home and shortly she was leaving her golf things in her garage and climbing the outside stairs to her apartment.

Several letters had been thrust under the door. She recognized one with her brother's writing and hastily took it to the nearest chair.

It was a nice, friendly letter, beginning with "Dear Lexi," and signed "Frank." And in the middle was an explanation for his long silence (he'd been into the interior of China looking for some lacquered chests). He said he hoped to be back in the States soon, but he had no idea when. However, he would come to Lookaway Mountain before he did anything else. He said he was sorry he hadn't been able to send any paintings this trip, but not one word did he write about Rosalyn.

It was perplexing. This was so different from the stilted typed letter in which he introduced his fiancée. Why didn't he say anything about her in this one? Was it because this letter had been mailed before he met Rosalyn? The mails to and from the Far East were irregular and perhaps that was the explanation. But why did he say that he was sorry he hadn't sent more paintings when there were four odious works in the closet that had come from him?

It was puzzling, but it had taken her mind off the happenings of the morning for a few minutes. The fear she'd experienced was in her still, but it was a fear that was healthily threaded with anger.

She included Keith in her ill will. He'd been sweet. He'd said he'd never hurt her. He'd tried to comfort her as well as warn her. He'd been gentlemanly about her atrocious game of golf. *But*—and there was a large but—he played a yellow ball and he could easily have been in the woods before joining her. Why would he try to pelt her with hurtful, dangerous golf balls? Tears would be a relief, but she had none to shed now. She was all too compellingly aware that her heart had gotten mixed up in the complications somehow.

Keith occupied her thoughts a great deal of the time, but she was finding that Jeff's lighthearted wooing had stopped being an annoyance and might well become a source of pleasure. She told herself that was a strange thing to be thinking after the morning's events.

All the same, Lexi closed her mind to her problems and took a cool bath.

Later that afternoon, Lexi had opened the gallery—even though it was Monday—and was puttering aimlessly in her workshop when the doorbell rang. Jeff walked inside.

"You've been gone for ages!" he accused her, melancholy in his voice. "I've been knocking at your door lo these many hours. Where were you? Don't you know my survival depends on seeing you at least once a day?"

"I played golf." Lexi smiled. "Very badly."

"Oh, well, then you can play with me tomorrow."

"I only play on Mondays, Jeff. It's the day I usually take off."

"Cruel! You are ruthless. Now let me tell you nobody's got more ruth than I, so I know!"

Lexi was laughing now. The man was an idiot but an entertaining one.

"You know, darling, your deep brown eyes are as clear as pebbles on the bottom of a stream. Lovely, quite lovely."

"Thanks, Jeff. Now tell me please, were you on the golf course early this morning, or rather, in the woods beside the first fairway?"

"Why, yes, how did you know? I get my jollies from never having to buy a golf ball. I get them the *hard* way. I *find* them."

"Jeff." She paused. "Jeff, what's your handicap?"

"A miserable eighteen. Why?"

Well, thought Lexi, that could let *him* out of my suspicions. He was not a good enough golfer to direct his shots accurately. Of course, he was strong enough to hit a lethal ball. No, she would not cross him off her list. Not yet.

A solid knot of stubbornness would have to substitute for courage, for she was determined to find her enemy.

She said, "Sit down," pointed to a bench by the wall, and seated herself behind the desk.

"Jeff?"

"Yes, my love."

"This morning someone shot golf balls at me, missing me by inches."

She saw Jeff's mouth drop open in exaggerated shock. Did he take nothing seriously?"

"Some kook practicing?" He frowned when he saw that Lexi was in earnest.

"No, definitely not. Whoever it was was hidden in the woods and was trying to hurt or frighten me. That's why I asked you if you were in the woods this morning."

"You suspect *me!* Your devoted slave? No, no, my sweet! My strength is as the strength of ten because my heart is pure. And, anyway, I wouldn't—couldn't—I mean..." He ran out of words in his indignation. He was incensed by the implications of her remarks and he no longer played the fool.

"If that's true," he said quietly, his face somber for once, "you can expect more harassment. Must you stay here? Can't you visit someone far away for a while?"

He was the second person to suggest she leave.

"No. I'm staying here. I've done nothing to anybody that would make them want to hurt me. And although I'm furious about being bombarded, I'm not really sure it was meant as an attack. I suppose it could have been an accident. Or some kid. Someone with a weird sense of humor, maybe."

Jeff looked cynical. "A perpetual innocent is a compulsive loser," he said. He sounded as though he were quoting someone else. He seemed almost to be talking to himself.

Then he asked the usual question. "How about dinner tonight?"

When Lexi said, "I'd love to," he looked so surprised she laughed.

They arranged to meet at the inn after Lexi had firmly turned down his offer to pick her up.

He left, whistling that very old song, "I Love You Truly."

Stone Mountain was etched in gold from the waning sun, and purple shadows fell across the road. How lovely a summer evening could be, Lexi thought as she closed the gallery and went up to dress. How pleasant to hear frogs gronking by the lake and tree creatures adding their chorus.

She was slightly surprised at herself for accepting Jeff's invitation to dinner, but in a way she was glad. Dressing up, dining, and chatting with a lighthearted, breezy young man would keep her thoughts and worries under control.

She selected a mint-green silk and added a silver belt for her slim waist, a silver necklace and earrings to match. The evening was warm, but she always felt deliciously cool in this particular outfit.

The first to greet her on the veranda of the inn was Rosalyn.

"Did you get a letter from your brother today, Alexis?" she asked.

"Yes. How did you know?"

"Because so did I. Frank will be here next week, I think. His letter was angry. He's mad because you wouldn't let me stay with you!"

How could Frank know that so soon? Lexi asked herself. It seemed impossible.

Chapter Five

Lexi stared at Rosalyn. The glow of happiness that had appeared when she'd heard Frank was coming was slowly fading. Rosalyn's further words killed the joy in Lexi's eyes; they had gone cold. She knew that Rosalyn was lying. First she doubted there had been enough time for Frank to learn about Rosalyn's visits to the gallery—and to respond in a letter. Also, it seemed unlikely Rosalyn had news of his arrival when his sister was kept in the dark. Frank just wouldn't treat Lexi that way.

So Frank's fiancée—or whatever she was—had to be lying.

Rosalyn's pretty face was alight with a lovely smile. "Frank wants you to meet him in Charleston," she went on. "You're to stay at the Golden Eagle and wait for him. I'll take care of the gallery for you, Alexis. What fun you'll have, dear! When will you leave?"

Lexi's impulse was to say "never," but she smiled back at the sleek auburn-haired girl. "How charming you look, Rosalyn! Your rust-colored outfit is perfect with your hair and eyes."

Rosalyn bent forward and placed a kiss on Lexi's smooth cheek. Lexi had been brought up to dislike being kissed by comparative strangers, for it seemed insincere. But she tried to hide her feelings.

Then she got back to the subject at hand. "As to my going to Charleston, I'm *not*."

"But, dearie, your only brother *wants* you! And your gallery will be completely safe in my hands," Rosalyn said.

"Thank you. Ah, here's Jeff! Jeff, I'm starving. Can we eat now?"

They left Rosalyn looking bemused.

Lexi said, "She's the third person to suggest I leave Lookaway Mountain for a while. What's the matter with everyone? Do you all think I'm so chicken that I run away from a couple of golf balls?"

"No doubt it's because we all have your well-being in mind, sweetheart. I'd feel more comfortable about you if you visited somewhere for a while. I'd probably pine away from not seeing you, but I'll sacrifice my feelings in exchange for your safety."

"Very kind," Lexi said, unmoved. "What do you know about Rosalyn?"

"She's attractive. Plays a whiz of a golf game. And—"

"And she's a liar!"

"Why, Lexi!" Jeff said.

"She is! Hey, there she is now with Bob. Oh, Rosalyn," Lexi called, "may I see the letter from Frank?"

"Sorry, Alexis. I've thrown it away."

"What did I tell you?" Lexi said softly to Jeff. "She won't show me the letter because there *isn't* one! She's a liar, but I don't understand why she's lying. I—I don't understand *any*thing that's been happening!" Tears pricked beneath her lids and she blinked rapidly.

Across the dining room, Lexi saw Keith. He was with two other men and, when he saw Lexi, he waved. Lexi hoped he'd come up to her, but he turned away. She felt an aching loss, but Jeff was talking his usual nonsense and she knew she must laugh or at least smile at him. Fortunately, he distracted her for most of the meal.

After a game of Bingo in the lounge, Jeff walked Lexi home. At the foot of her outside stairs, he kissed her lightly.

"Your lips are as soft as rose petals, Lexi," he whispered. Then he took her in his arms rather forcefully, and his next kiss was more demanding. But brief.

She had felt herself melting, being captivated, almost entranced by that kiss that had ended so soon.

He departed abruptly, leaving her dismayed and a little hurt. Why *should* she be hurt? she asked herself. She was definitely not interested in him. Definitely not.

You're awfully mixed up, girl, aren't

you? Lexi thought as she slowly climbed the stairs and unlocked the door. When she was with Keith, she had emotions that could be explained only if she admitted to being in love with him. But now Jeff's kiss had unsettled her and she didn't know who she was in love with.

How frivolous! She had several serious problems and she shouldn't be wasting time on trifling, silly, piddling dreams of love. Gloom entered her soul.

Lexi couldn't sleep. Night thoughts are bad—problems become bigger, insoluble. Her depression deepened. Something very strange was happening, and she began to wonder if her brother might be mixed up in it somehow. Then things sort of whirled around in her head.

The golf balls as weapons—the paintings in the closet—Frank's letter to her that didn't mention Rosalyn or the bad paintings he'd sent—Rosalyn's obvious lies—everybody wanting her to leave the gallery—Jeff's kiss—Keith's cold gray eyes—Jeff's clowning—Keith's concern...

Her heart was thumping uncomfortably against her ribs and her mouth was dry. She left her bed and went to the kitchen for a glass of milk. She must make her thoughts behave.

There was a slight rattle from her garbage can outside. That cat again?

Lexi stole very quietly to the door, unbolted it, and crept out to the landing. There was a shape bending over the can that definitely was not feline. Unfortunately, the moon was obscured by black clouds and Lexi couldn't see clearly.

"What do you want?" she called. "Who are you?" And she had the unclear picture of a human figure as it scuttled into the shadows.

Had she lived in the city where there was poverty and hunger, there would have been an explanation for the rifling of her garbage can. But what on earth could anyone here want with her rubbish? She tried to remember what was in the can. Some junk mail, some empty frozen-food cartons, some orange peel, some coffee grounds in a plastic sack, an old dustcloth—and the wrappings of the last two paintings Frank had sent. Could they be the attraction, the magnet that drew someone to her trash? Was there something valuable about the wrappings? Or any of the other garbage? In the morning she would go through the debris.

When Lexi awoke the next day the sky was the color of iron, and soon a dense fog crept in. The weather was not conducive to any outdoor activity. From her windows, it was barely possible to see across the road, and the dark whiteness of the fog blotted out all signs of the inn. She would wait, she told herself, till the fog lifted before examining her trash. Why must she examine it, anyway? she pondered. She knew very well what the can contained. Would it solve any problems to sift through that stuff? Probably not, but later on she'd take a look, anyway. She had a nagging unease about it.

She rather liked a foggy or rainy day. It wasn't good for business, but she loved puttering around her back room, fixing frames or cutting mats, or trying her hand at painting or modeling in clay. Also, she was going to take another look, a more thorough look, at the four awful paintings in the closet. Was it possible that those dreadful works had something to do with all the strange happenings lately?

Around ten o'clock the fog still blanketed the area, and it was damp and chilly.

Lexi, dressed warmly in tan corduroy slacks and a light sweater, finished cleaning up her apartment. Today she would light a fire in the stove that heated the back room. On chilly days both the gallery and her apartment were warmed by electricity in concealed tubes around the floorboards. But the back room had drafts, and a stove was quite necessary there at times.

She wished a niggling little fear would go away. There was absolutely *nothing* to be afraid of, she told herself. And yet...

She had to feel her way down the stairs and around to the door of the gallery. She'd never seen fog so thick. Once she was inside, warmth greeted her and she discarded her raincoat.

First things first, she told herself, even before she lit the stove. She had no desire to re-examine the four paintings in the closet, but she wanted to get it over with.

The closet was big. The sides were lined with canvas stretchers, mat boards, lengths of frame molding, and a few light-weight easels. There was a light overhead with a string dangling, and Lexi noted that the bulb would soon need to be replaced. It was flickering.

She reached behind some mat boards and brought out the hideous paintings. That pink poodle was heavy. Did acrylic paint laid on as lavishly as this always weigh a ton? She was surprised she hadn't noticed the heaviness before, but then she'd been too preoccupied by the bubble-gum quality of the picture. She gathered up the others and was about to leave the closet for better light when the closet door closed.

Darn. A draft. Lexi put down the paintings and turned the knob on the closet door. Nothing happened. She tried again, only to realize she was locked in. And she knew that the lock was not automatic. The key had to be turned in the keyhole and the key could only be turned by human hands.

There was someone out there in her

back room. Someone who had locked Lexi in either on purpose or by accident.

"Please," she called, "let me out!" A chill of fear ran down her spine.

Was there a chuckle coming from under the door? Could this be a practical joke? Or was it a deliberate attempt to frighten her? If it were the latter, the attempt was succeeding. She was conscious of a growing uneasiness prickling under her skin, and she fought encroaching panic.

"Please!" Lexi called. "Enough is enough! I don't like it in here!"

Faint noises were coming through the door. The light bulb above her flared up and died. The dark was intense.

"Whoever you are," she called bravely, "you've proven your point. I'm a silly coward. Now let me out! I promise to take it as a joke."

Her stomach pitched down and came slowly up again as it always does when hope departs. Her enemy was out there and was not about to free her. The pelting golf balls were part of some sinister scheme that made no sense at all. What next? Lexi shivered. It was cold in the closet, and terror was close.

"At least you can light the wood-burning stove," she cried. "That's unless you plan to deep-freeze me." Her voice wavered.

Silence answered her. Had her enemy left? Left her imprisoned and cold? But then she heard a rustle of paper and tried to believe it was the starting of the fire in the stove.

But minutes later there were no crackles of burning wood, and no heat seeped under the door to comfort her. The enemy was only going through her equipment—rummaging around her painting gear and probably messing up her supplies.

Lexi pressed her lips tight in a determined effort to pull herself together. She was not going to let this person cow her. Eventually, she'd be let out—she hoped—and in the meantime she'd keep her teeth from chattering. And when the enemy unlocked the door to see if she was still alive or had suffocated to death, she'd hit him with a canvas stretcher.

Did that sound suspiciously like *The Little Engine That Could?* Well, she just had to make an effort to protect herself, didn't she?

Now Lexi heard definite noises—the opening and closing of the gallery door—and a moist draft crept around her feet. Had her adversary gone off and left her locked up? Tears were like hot needles behind her eyes. A sob escaped her, then another.

"Lexi?" a male voice called. "Lexi, are you here?"

"Oh, please," she cried, "let me out! Please!"

In a minute she heard the key scrape in the keyhole, and blessed light stole into the closet.

"What are you doing in there?" Keith asked. "How come you were locked in?"

She couldn't answer. Not yet. She just sagged toward him and felt his arms go around her. She met his kiss with hers. But then, in a moment of clarity, she realized that he might very well have been the one who had imprisoned her. He might be pretending to have just entered the gallery whereas in reality he'd opened and closed the door to disguise his having been here all along. A small, angry flame leapt inside her and she pushed him away.

"Well," Keith said, "the greeting, short as it was, was quite satisfactory. If only it could be repeated! If only all kisses were as welcome as that was! If only you'd explain why you pushed me away and are now glaring at me! And if only you'd get around to telling me what you were doing inside a locked closet!"

"Stop saying, 'if only,'" she said crossly.

"We all carry a pack of 'if onlys' around on our breaking backs. Now tell me about it and wipe the tears from your shockingly beautiful eyes."

Lexi looked around the back room and saw that many of her working tools were disturbed. In the gallery almost all of the paintings were hanging crooked. They'd been taken down, examined, and quickly hung up again. Nothing seemed to be missing.

If her enemy had been a thief, a knowledgeable thief, he'd have stolen the Robert Alton landscape and the Carroll Rivers wildflowers. But they were both safely though crookedly hanging on the wall.

"What were you looking for?" Lexi asked Keith coldly.

"What do you mean?"

"I mean, when you locked me up and examined every painting in the gallery and messed up all my equipment in the back room."

Keith looked aghast. "You think that *I—I* would do such a thing? Why, Lexi, I'd be the last one to do such a thing!"

"Don't you 'Why, Lexi' me! You told me yesterday that you were looking for something, but it was mean and sneaky to lock me up. If you'd only asked me, I'd have shown you whatever you want."

Keith took her by the shoulders and briefly shook her. He shook her again and ended up by kissing her. It was a kiss that shook her up more than his shaking had done. It was a kiss never to be forgotten, and Lexi felt the bubble of dark suspicion burst. Keith couldn't kiss like that if he were guilty. She let herself relax and returned the kiss with all her heart.

They were both breathless when at last

they were out of each other's arms.

Keith looked at Lexi tenderly. "Now will you explain?"

"When you came in, did anyone go out?" Lexi asked. "You see, there was someone, my enemy, who sneaked in, locked me up, then started searching for something. What was he looking for, Keith?"

Keith shook his head.

Lexi persisted. "I might be able to help you if I knew what you're searching for."

"Nobody went out as I came in, Lexi, but the front door wasn't entirely closed. Someone could have left in a hurry and was immediately hidden by the fog. As for what we're looking for, I suppose you deserve to know. Stolen gold coins of great value and smuggled jewels, all unset and some uncut."

"Oh, Keith, I haven't any idea where such loot could be. I only know nothing in my gallery or apartment could possibly conceal jewels or gold coins. You're free to look. Where would you like to begin?"

Lexi had a terrible feeling that if he took up her offer to search the place, it meant he didn't trust her. It would mean that the kiss was false, that his tenderness had been a ploy to soften her resistance. She felt desolate and was conscious of a loneliness that was accentuated by Keith's devious brain.

"Go ahead," she said coldly.

Keith made a quick examination of the gallery, then went into the back room. It was already in disarray from the previous ransacker. He pawed through her equipment, shaking his head. He looked into the closet and pulled the light cord.

When no light came on, he said, "Got a flashlight?"

"No."

"I'll come back with one, dear girl."

Lexi felt dismal. She had no tolerance for this "dear girl" stuff. Her lips stretched into a facsimile of a smile.

"Are you ready to snoop in my apartment now? Here's the key. Have a happy investigation."

She felt so numbed she hardly heard his footsteps as he climbed the outside stairs. And when she heard a distant whistle coming nearer, she failed to recognize the tune at first. Then she realized it was "I Love You Truly." That meant Jeff was coming.

But she was sorely disappointed that Keith had so little faith in her. That he should search for contraband in her home made her especially miserable. And that misery added to her fear was more than she could bear.

Chapter Six

It was not only Jeff who entered the gallery. Rosalyn was clinging to his arm and making kitten-like mewlings about how wet and uncomfortable she was.

"Give me your coat," Lexi said. "I'll lend you a dry one when you leave in a few minutes."

"But I'm not leaving in a few minutes," Rosalyn said.

"Yes, you are."

"How impolite!" Jeff said. "Here comes this poor girl through the foggy, foggy dew to get to know your gallery better, so she

80

can take over when you go to meet your brother. And how do you react? Do I hear footsteps overhead?"

Lexi ignored him. She was annoyed. Her initial pleasure at Jeff's arrival was spoiled by Rosalyn's unwanted presence. And the assumption both Jeff and Rosalyn had made that she was going to depart and leave the gallery in Rosalyn's care was beyond belief. Disillusioned as she was with Keith's perfidy, she wanted him to come down and be with her.

Meanwhile, there was brittle, empty, superficial conversation between Jeff and Rosalyn. They sat stiffly on the bench and cast their eyes at the ceiling as heavy footsteps resounded.

"Cigarette?" Jeff asked.

"No thank you," Rosalyn said.

"Mind if I do?"

"Not at all."

How polite they were, Lexi thought. How discreet they believed themselves to be, not to question the footsteps overhead.

Finally, Lexi laughed.

"It's Keith," she said. "He's looking for something. I have the feeling you two are both looking for something, too. You're all-fired anxious to have me go away, and I'm beginning to think it's because you'd then be free to search this place. It's been done already, you know. At least, *one* of you knows."

"What can you mean, Alexis dear?" Rosalyn asked.

Lexi didn't answer because she heard Keith coming down the stairs, and in a minute he entered the door.

"I *thought* I heard voices," Keith said, shaking the moisture from his shoulders, "and I couldn't believe Lexi was talking to herself. How are you both? Miserable weather, isn't it?"

Lexi stood up. "I assume you did not find what you were looking for," she said to Keith. Her voice was chilly. "If you all will excuse me now, I'll light the fire in the stove."

"Let me help you, sweetheart," Jeff said.

"All right. And then I'm going to show you something that just might be what you're all looking for. When the fire's lit, we'll go into the back room."

Rosalyn looked bored. She shivered delicately. "It's the damp more than the cold that's so chilling. It seems to penetrate the bones."

Pretty soon the fire in the stove danced, wrapping greedy tongues of flame around the pine logs.

Lexi cleared camp chairs and stools and invited the others in. She was taking a chance with what she planned to show them. It seemed incredible, but the idea had come to her while Keith had searched her apartment. If she was wrong, she'd be laughed at, but that mattered very little.

"Tell me," Rosalyn said, "do you always keep this room so messy?"

"Yes, indeed," Lexi answered. "Don't you think the mess gives an air of artistic turmoil? Creative people never have time to tidy up their surroundings, you know. They're too busy trying to illuminate and define the underlying order beneath this human chaos."

Not for worlds was Lexi going to tell this rude young woman that it was a ransacker who had messed it up. And, anyway, there was no proof it hadn't been Rosalyn who had done it.

Lexi went to the closet and in the dimness she identified the pink poodle by its weight.

She brought it out and put it on an easel.

There were gasps and murmurs and eager eyes.

"That's the dog I've been after," Jeff said. "I'll buy it."

"It's not for sale. I refuse to handle it. It's my brother's problem."

"May I inspect it?" Keith asked. "Heavens, isn't it horrible? But maybe it has some underlying value."

"You don't want to keep such a frightful painting in your lovely gallery," Rosalyn said. "I can get rid of it for you."

"Thank you, but no thank you. Frank sent it and, until he comes and decides what to do with it, it stays here."

Keith was standing by the easel. He lifted the painting, turned it upside down and backward. "It weighs a ton," he said. "and I have reason to believe it really is valuable."

"Never mind that," Lexi said. "You've all seen it now and I seem to gather it's what you were searching for."

She lifted it and carried it back to the closet.

Jeff groaned, "It's just what I want!"

Keith had a puzzled, worried expression on his face, and Rosalyn looked furtive.

Lexi now brought out the painting of the Oriental temple. For a moment nobody seemed interested. Then Jeff examined the frame and his eyes grew large.

"I could swear," he said, "it's made of—"

"Let me see!" Rosalyn snatched it from him.

"It's not a good painting, so there must be something of value to it," Keith said as he bent over Rosalyn. "Lexi, have you got any more secrets?"

"Yes, two more. You want to see them?"

Lexi was torn between exasperation and interest. She hated the avaricious looks in their eyes as they scrutinized the tasteless paintings, but now she could understand that there was monetary value of one kind or another in each dreadful work of art.

She took the temple from Rosalyn's grasp and tucked it away with the poodle in the closet. She was averse to showing the two remaining works, but she had offered to display them and felt she should. Lexi next chose the cat with the plastic eyes and glass beads pasted to it.

"Oh! Oh, oh!" Rosalyn exclaimed. "I must have him! He's perfect, he's just what I've been hoping for! Alexis, how much are you asking?"

"He's not for sale, either."

"Do you know what the eyes are, Lexi?" Keith asked when he had closely scanned the atrocious piece.

"No. Are they valuable?"

"They are. Do either of you recognize what the eyes are?" Keith asked Jeff and Rosalyn.

Rosalyn pretended indifference, but Jeff expressed curiosity.

"They're fire opals," Keith said. "Well-disguised by a sheet of plastic. And the cat's necklace! Good heavens! Do you know what that is?"

But Lexi took the cat painting away from him. "That's enough," she said. "I don't want to know any more."

"But *we* do, sweetie!" Rosalyn said. "This is fascinating!"

Jeff's expression had a hungering, hankering look.

Rosalyn looked crafty, and Keith looked worried. "Are there more?" he asked Lexi.

"One more, but I don't feel like taking it out just now."

"Oh, please! You can't stop now!" Rosalyn said.

"Yes, I can. And I think it's time for you all to leave."

"Lexi," Jeff said, "we can't leave you alone with all this stuff. You don't know who might try to take it from you."

"You mean someone like you?" Lexi's voice was severe.

"Jeff is right," Keith said. "You may have a fortune here, and you could be in danger because of it."

"And so," Lexi said, "you want to relieve me of it for my own benefit, of course!" Her sarcasm was quite clear. She tried to look cool and composed, but her heart was bumping noisily.

There was tenseness in every line of her

body, and she talked rapidly now and in fits and starts. "If you think I don't appreciate your kindly concern, you're right! I don't! You're one of a kind, all out to plunder and bamboozle. These paintings, bad as they are—and valuable as they may be—are my brother's, and they stay here until he comes. Now please go."

"Do you know you're saying your brother is a smuggler?" Keith said. "Maybe a thief?"

"Get out! Go away and don't come back! I never want to see any of you ever again!" Lexi said.

She herded them out of the gallery, paying no attention to their protests of innocence and offers of guardianship, and locked the door behind them.

Hatred for the three of them constricted her muscles, cramped her stomach, and tightened her chest until she thought she might suffocate. She forced herself to breathe slowly, but there was no way she could still the pounding of her heart. Oh, Frank, she thought, please hurry back! I need you. And please, please don't be involved in anything criminal. Please!

The fog lifted, but the change in weather was not for the better. The sky turned from a dull leaden gray to a muted brownish gray. The landscape was tinted in shades of sepia, ecru, and beige.

Lexi had had her fill of the gallery and the back room. The morning was only half gone, but the prospect of painting or modeling in clay had lost its charm. She needed to be alone, alone in her pretty, soothing apartment where she could sort out her thoughts.

She locked the storage closet and put the key in her pocket. she hung a sign in the window that said the gallery was closed. She locked up the gallery and ran up the outside stairs to her sanctuary.

For a long time Lexi sat by her picture window and stared out at Stone Mountain as she considered her problems. She would have gone to the sheriff by now if she weren't worried about Frank and what he might have to do with this mess. Not that he could be guilty of anything. But she must not do anything brash before he returned.

Lexi sighed. She had come so close to

falling in love with Keith, and she had been attracted to Jeff's breeziness. But both men had proved themselves so easily overwhelmed by a possible monetary gain—and had the effrontery to suggest she wasn't capable of being custodian of the frightful paintings.

Then what Keith had said about her brother! That he might be a smuggler or a thief! Oh, surely, that couldn't be true!

And now the moaning of a sudden wind and the subsequent hammering of rain seemed to undermine what reserves of courage Lexi had.

Oh, Frank, Frank, she thought, *I* know you're not a thief! You couldn't be! You're my sweet, considerate, decent brother, my only family, the only one I can trust! But please come home quick and help me clean up this mess!

She didn't cry hard. She just let the depression have its way, and sad tears flowed warm and soft down her cheeks.

There was a knock on her door.

"Who is it?"

"It's Jeff, darling. May I come in for a while?"

"Go away!"

"Please, Lexi, we have to talk!"

"No we don't."

"I have a message from Bob at the inn. He suggested a picnic for tomorrow."

"Great," Lexi scoffed. "There's nothing I'd rather do than go on a picnic in weather like this!"

"He promises hot, clear weather for to-morrow. Please, sweetheart, you mustn't take on like this."

"I've got a date for tomorrow," she said, lying without hesitation.

"Lexi, you mustn't think I'm with the others. They're plotters, as you know. They plan to deprive you of—of—well, what-ever. Not me. My life's an open book. May I come in?"

Lexi decided she'd been moping by her-self long enough. Jeff was sometimes amusing and she dearly needed a laugh.

"Oh, all right," she said. She unbolted the door and took Jeff's raincoat.

"What a pretty place," he said. "I love blue and white."

Lexi smiled. She couldn't quite hate someone who admired her taste.

The door wasn't all the way closed, and an extraordinary chorus from lakeside frogs could be heard. The rain had inspired them to outdo their gronking selves.

Lexi laughed. "Do you think they have fleas?" she asked, cocking her head toward the door.

"I think they're having a nervous breakdown," Jeff replied. "And talking of breakdowns, I thought you might have one earlier today. Poor, lovely thing, you were shaken, weren't you, by the three of us acting like criminals or spies?"

Lexi nodded. "You all were horrid!"

"Yes, we were. I apologize for my own behavior. And you were quite right in sending us away."

She sighed. "I'm sorry if I behaved badly, but I've had a rough day. And my nerves were in such shreds from everybody's greed, I couldn't think clearly."

Jeff put his arms around her, but for some reason the act failed to give her pleasure or comfort. She pushed him away.

"Now about tomorrow," Jeff said, apparently not at all disturbed by her rejection of him, "may I tell Bob you'll come? It's to be a swimming, fishing, hiking picnic. And aside from the four of us— meaning you, me, Rosalyn, and Keith— there'll be Bob and two couples who are staying at the inn."

"You think the rain will stop?" Lexi asked.

"Bob guarantees a beautiful, sunny day."

"All right. I guess I can close the gallery tomorrow. What time?"

They discussed the time, what to wear, what to bring, and as she led Jeff out to the landing of her stairs, she saw the rain had stopped.

Lexi felt better for his visit and fixed herself a fried-egg sandwich and a glass of milk. She might as well re-open the gallery now that there was no more rain— especially since she was closing it tomorrow. Her conscience wouldn't bother her quite as much if it were open now.

She was glad she'd made that decision. Three people came in, browsed, and bought two Japanese prints. Then a man with a beard bought a small oil for his wife's birthday, and another potential buyer promised to return next week.

It was a good afternoon.

At eleven o'clock, Lexi went to bed, but an hour later she was still awake and moonlight was slanting through the windows and casting long, elegant shadows on the walls. Bob's prediction of good weather was coming true. The picnic might be fun. At least she would try not to carry her worries along, and Keith would be there. Did she care whether he was or not? Did she? Pondering that question, Lexi fell asleep.

She awoke suddenly. The wind was whispering at the windows and it was pitch dark. She sat up, listening. Something had awakened her. That cat again? Or that skulking figure by the trash can? Or—or something more deadly?

Chapter Seven

Lexi's mind went into high speed. Now that she knew her storage closet held valuables, she realized, every sound could mean that a burglar had slyly invaded her house. She had the key to the closet. The gallery was locked. And there was nothing further she could do. Until Frank came home. Then they would no doubt confer with the sheriff.

Meanwhile, though, she really mustn't become a nervous Nellie, jumping at every noise and suspecting the worst. She would put her mind on tomorrow's picnic, or was it today's? If Bob was right and it was sunny and hot, she would wear a bathing suit under her blue jeans and possibly carry shorts in a tote bag. Maybe the picnic would be fun. Again she fell asleep.

When Lexi awoke, the sun was streaming in her windows, and a glance at her clock told her that if she didn't hurry she'd be late.

A half hour later she was on the inn's veranda greeting Bob and meeting the two couples who were going to go along. One couple, the Terrys, were in their seventies. The other couple, the Blacks, looked to be in their thirties. All of them were very pleasant and friendly.

Lexi had rushed to get there, skipping breakfast and not entering her gallery, and so she was considerably put out by Rosalyn's tardiness that held up the group. Keith had made his appearance soon after Lexi had arrived, and then Jeff strolled up, hands in pockets and whistling.

Fifteen minutes passed before Rosalyn appeared. Her sleek auburn hair and striking topaz eyes and the jangle of her bracelets did nothing to make Lexi more tolerant. She just couldn't stand the woman.

Everything about Rosalyn was an irritant. Her smile looked as if it had been pasted on her pretty face. And when Keith sidled up to her, insisting she sit beside him in the minibus that was to take them to Mirror Lake, Lexi felt her annoyance build to the summit. Be honest, she told herself. Admit it. You're jealous. Even though you don't trust or really like Keith, you don't want him to be attracted to Rosalyn. Admit it and live with it and try to laugh it off. Don't let it fester.

Jeff was beside Lexi in the bus, and she let him hold her hand. There was some comfort in having his lighthearted wooing at a time when she felt insecure. Jealousy and insecurity went hand in hand, she knew. If she thought it a bit odd to be with Jeff and Keith and Rosalyn after yesterday, she quickly forced herself to forget it.

Rosalyn was being very elfin and animated, and Bob was loaded with heavy-handed courtliness for all the ladies. Lexi was glad when the minibus pulled up beside a thick growth of rhododendron and they all piled out.

The large picnic hampers, ice chests, fishing gear, and charcoal were picked up and carried by the men along the woodland path to the lakeshore.

This territory was unfamiliar to Lexi. She had heard of Mirror Lake, driven past the turnoff to it, but had never ventured in as far as the lake. It was an enchanting spot, lovely in its isolation and unspoiled perfection. Not a single cottage could be seen in any direction. And the sparkling water seemed coolly inviting.

"Shall we swim first or hike?" Bob asked.

"Let's swim. The sun is hot now and may not be later," Rosalyn said.

"I'm going to walk along the edge and find me a place to fish," Mr. Black said. Mr. Terry decided to do likewise, and their two wives opted to read in the shade.

Rosalyn had her bikini on under her slacks and top. Her figure, Lexi hated to admit, was on the gorgeous side. That might be why Frank had fallen for her.

Lexi watched in a sort of morbid fasci-
nation as the woman dove from a high
rock into the lake with the oiled perfection of a dolphin.

"Golly, how beautiful!" Jeff said. "I admire anyone who can cleave the water
without a ripple."

Keith and Bob were all admiring eyes,
too, and Lexi was so provoked she threw
off her outer clothes, climbed the rock,
and jumped—her legs and arms all askew
to make as much splash as possible.

Keith and Jeff followed her, laughing
and competing as to who could make the
loudest commotion in hitting the water.

Lexi's ploy had paid off. She'd started a
fun contest and Rosalyn's perfection was
forgotten.

They wallowed and raced and did stunts
in the clear water while Bob lit the charcoal and got out the makings for drinks.
The fishermen finally wandered back as
aromas from the fire got to them, and their
wives joined the group. Lexi and Rosalyn
went behind a clump of rhododendron and
changed.

It was a gourmet picnic and everybody ate to excess. Then all but Lexi, Keith, and Rosalyn elected to snooze off the meal. Lexi said she thought she'd walk around the lake. Rosalyn said there was a path going off to the right she'd like to explore and asked Keith if he'd go with her.

Lexi looked at Keith, who was still in his trunks. The outline of his rib cage was handsomely coated with bronzed skin. He was beautiful!

When he agreed to go with Rosalyn, Lexi felt an annoying surge of self-pity. It was her own fault, though, wasn't it? She'd made Keith realize that he wasn't welcome in her presence anymore. How was he to know that despite all her doubts, she wanted him to be as friendly as before. Friendly? Was that what she wanted? She must stop kidding herself. Whatever she did, she mustn't lie to herself. It hurt to see Keith being bewitched by Frank's fiancée.

Lexi's mind closed quickly, obliterating that train of thought before it raced too far in its painful direction.

In the woods it was cool and shadowy after the shimmering brilliance of the lake. Lexi hurried away from the others. The tears of frustration were like hot needles behind her eyes.

It was getting late and she had gone halfway around the lake before she thought she heard footsteps behind her, but when she stopped to listen, there was nothing but the thick silence of the forest.

Then came the words that were still and soft, the disembodied voice a genderless whisper in the silent woods. "You're in danger, Alexis. You have an enemy."

"What did you say?" Lexi called. "I can't make out what you said. Who are you? Come closer—don't act like a phantom!" She made her own voice as hearty as possible even though she was shaking inside. "Please, who are you? Mineral, vegetable, or animal?" she added, hoping to make herself *and* the phantom believe she was only amused by the ghostly voice in the sunset.

But there was no answer. A slight rustling in the undergrowth could have been made by a startled animal—Lexi was convinced it wasn't.

Suddenly, she was frightened and ran. Panic, unreasoning dread, made her breath come fast, made her hurtle over and through bushes, bumping into trees and stumbling over rocks. Branches scratched her face and twigs broke off in her hair.

A crippling stitch in her side made her stop. For a minute she was motionless, and when she could continue, she looked for the lake. It was not in sight. She was lost!

Dusk was approaching. The sky was slightly sinister; gray, rose, mauve, and deep purple accented the clouds. Was it going to rain again? That possibility made Lexi fight to control the hysteria that was surging through her body. Her legs were shaking and she panted painfully. The stitch came back. There seemed to be a large splinter sticking into her side. Which direction should she take to find the lake?

But now her thoughts were quickening, gathering speed and clarity. What a fool she'd been losing herself and imagining terrible things just because she'd heard a voice. Or *thought* she'd heard it. The way to the lake had to be to the right, and once she was at the lake, she could call to the others or just continue all around it until she reached the picnic spot. She must not lose her head again.

All at once, she heard someone whistle a familiar song: "I Love You Truly."

"Jeff," she called, "oh, Jeff, I'm over here!"

But the whistle faded. Could Jeff have been the whisperer who had frightened her? Anger now supplanted the fear and she trudged onward hoping that the direction the whistle came from was the right one.

She had a strange feeling of unreality, as if she were in the landscape of a dream. Being lost was a little scary, but a warning whisper was *really* frightening, no matter what she'd tried to tell herself a few minutes before. She knew she'd be found by the others if she didn't find her own way. But there was no one Lexi could turn to about the warning. Rosalyn and Keith and Jeff were all suspect. And she did not want to bother Bob or the other two couples with it.

Suddenly, a figure stepped out from a thicket in front of her. Lexi gasped in terror.

"What's the matter with you, Lexi?" It was Keith.

She said, "Oh, I've never been so glad to see anyone in my life!" Then she added, "I'm lost!"

"No, you're not! The rest of the group are within fifty feet of you, silly! Listen! You hear them talking, don't you?"

His arms were quickly around her, holding her close. He kissed her gently, but her lips were cool and unresponsive. She had suddenly thought that it might have been Keith who had whispered.

But then he said, "I love you, dammit!"

Lexi choked, but managed to murmur, "Why dammit?"

"Because I've tried for days to say those words!"

Her lips became soft and warm and melded to his. Her heart was beating fast and her whole body was suffused with tenderness.

"Why," she whispered when she'd recovered the use of her voice, "did you go off with Rosalyn? Why did you ask her to sit with you in the bus? Why didn't you ask *me?*"

"I wanted to, but Rosalyn wouldn't let me. The venom in her was running over, and I thought it better for you if I complied with her wishes. Though why she wanted me, I don't know."

There was an awkward silence between them that began to lengthen unbearably.

"I see," Lexi said stiffly, although she saw only that Keith was exaggerating. No doubt he had exaggerated his declaration of love, too. Her heart had stopped thumping with joy. It was slowly tolling the death of hope.

Keith lifted her chin, wanting to kiss her again, but she resisted.

He said, "Please?"

As ungraciously as possible, she said, "Oh, all right, but make it quick!"

Keith looked at her in astonishment. He didn't kiss her. His hand dropped from her chin. He shrugged. He scowled and, finally, he turned away from her, saying, "Follow me."

In a matter of minutes they were back at the picnic site.

"Had a nice walk?" Bob asked.

"Oh, great! The woods whisper sweet nothings, the paths disappear, I got lost," Lexi rattled on, listening to herself with a mild disbelief and a rising hysteria.

"I see you had company to get lost with," Rosalyn said, waving a graceful hand at Keith. "No wonder you were so late in joining the rest of us."

Jeff spoke up. "Everybody likes to believe the worst because the worst is always more exciting than the best."

Keith had moved away from Lexi. Her heart sank even further. Theirs had been the shortest romance in history. Of course, she was at fault, she thought. But couldn't he know instinctively that—under her doubts and fears—she cared for him? Oh, what was the use? He was back at Rosalyn's side.

I've blown it, she told herself. The ache

in her heart was not subsiding. Her eyes were bright with unshed tears, but she refused to let them flow.

Instead, Lexi became irritable and longed to throw something at somebody, preferably at Rosalyn. But there'd be satisfaction in throwing something at Keith, too. He really could try the patience of an angel. Not that she was an angel, she admitted to herself.

Clay and Susan Black, the couple in their thirties, were holding hands and murmuring to each other. To a lover who has given up hope, Lexi mused, the happiness of others is painful.

Keith strode purposefully up to Lexi. "Come with me," he said.

Lexi nodded and followed him.

He took her only a few yards away, out of hearing range of the others, and said, "Rosalyn is an angry woman, and angry women are dangerous, Lexi."

"That makes two of us."

"In case you don't know, she's angry because you won't let her roam around in your gallery where she can go over those terrible paintings at leisure. She's mad because you wouldn't sell her the cat painting. She's eaten up with jealousy because both Jeff and I are more attracted to you than to her. There's probably more, but that's enough."

Lexi looked at Keith with large eyes. "Do you mean it? That I attract you more than she does?"

"Oh, go to the devil!" he snapped.

Lexi was pleased by his wicked words. They showed that he really was attracted to her.

Still, could she fully trust this unpredictable young man?

Chapter Eight

It was late and Lexi was tired when she arrived back at her apartment. She planned on a light snack and an early bedtime. Tomorrow was soon enough to go to her gallery. A few more hours of neglect wouldn't hurt it.

Lexi wanted terribly to relax and find peace of mind, but that same mind kept being vibrantly alive, thoughts milling through it.

She lay wide-eyed in the night. Her eyes were dry, but tears were inside her. Oh, for an uncomplicated love! To be able to love without suspicion would be so heavenly.

She wondered if anything wonderful would ever happen to her. She had a dreary picture of herself trying to sell paintings year after year.

She'd never thought her life would turn out this way. For as long as she could remember, Lexi had had a belief that something marvelous lay in store for her. But here she was, twenty-four years old, and whatever this great thing was, it hadn't happened yet. Unless it was Keith. Keith, oh, Keith.

Unexpectedly she fell asleep.

Lexi felt wonderful the next morning, all her worries miraculously put aside and the hope that she'd see Keith high in her thoughts.

At breakfast some of her fears came back to torment her. But she vowed to be brave, no matter what.

Well, anyway, it was to be a good day— she felt it in her bones. So later when the gallery doorbell rang and a plump woman entered and immediately decided she'd buy Lexi's own painting, which hung inconspicuously under the Rivers, she was not completely surprised.

"You look too pretty to be an artist," the plump woman said when she heard Lexi was the one who'd painted her picture. "Most of them seem to wear last year's gunny sacks!"

Yes, it was going to be a good day.

Several other visitors came in. One of them came to claim his "lay-away" work of art and pay the balance. Another expressed interest in a rather moody rendition of Stone Mountain. He didn't buy but said he'd be back.

Lexi was tidying the back room when the bell rang again.

She called, "I'll be right with you!"

"You will, will you?" answered a familiar voice, a dear and long-awaited voice.

"Frank! Oh, Frank!" Lexi burst into tears of sheer relief as she flew to him.

"Well!" He lightly kissed the top of her head. "It's a surprise when my sister goes into hysterics at the sight of me!"

He was laughing as he helped Lexi mop up her face. "Why so emotional, Lex?"

"I'm sorry, Frank! I've been longing for your return! Well, Rosalyn was right when she said you'd be here soon."

"Who's Rosalyn?" he asked.

"Don't you know?"

"No. Why would someone named Rosalyn know when I was coming back?"

"Rosalyn is your fiancée, or had you forgotten?"

Frank stared at his sister. "My fiancée? Rosalyn?" he said. "I don't know what you're talking about. Better start from the beginning, slowly and clearly, Lexi. Let's sit on the bench."

Dry-eyed now and trying to grasp the fact that her brother was here and was telling her that the name Rosalyn meant nothing to him, Lexi told him of Rosalyn's introduction to her by a letter supposedly from *him*. Her nervousness made her speak a little fast, and Frank took hold of one of her hands.

"Steady, old girl. What you're saying is of great importance, so don't skip and don't hurry. I want to meet this Rosalyn."

"Oh, and, Frank, the last four paintings you sent me—the temple, the poodle, the cat, and the abstract—did you know that they are terribly valuable? Not as art, but—"

"Lexi, I think you've gone nuts! I haven't sent you paintings for at least seven months!"

"Come with me, Frank. I've got them locked up in the storage closet. My friends—at least they pretend to be my friends—and Rosalyn, too, all went mad with greed when I showed them the paintings. Come on!"

She led Frank into the back and unlocked the closet.

A sharp inhalation burst from her. The paintings were gone.

Frank supported her to the nearest camp chair.

She was incoherent with shock. "Stolen, Frank! They've been stolen! I heard a funny noise the night before last, but I didn't come in here yesterday because I was at a picnic. Well, Keith told me a while ago he was looking for illegal valuables and—"

"Slow down, Lex, you're overwrought. Now describe the paintings. First tell me where they were sent from."

Lexi looked at him in confusion. "Why, I only know they were from somewhere in the Orient. I didn't check the outside. I thought they were from you." She looked up hopefully. "I'll go look in the trash, Frank. The wrapping from the last one, the cat, might still be there."

"I'll go with you. Now calm down, dear."

He helped Lexi up and they were walking toward the front door when it opened.

Rosalyn walked in. "Oh, you've got company, Alexis," she said. She was beautiful, immaculately groomed, and shining, with her hair brushed smooth. "Do introduce us, Alexis," she added. "He's the best-looking man I've ever seen!"

Frank's face reddened. Lexi couldn't tell whether it was from anger or embarrassment.

"I can't think of anything of less importance," he said stiffly.

"Rosalyn," Lexi said slowly and calculatedly, "this is your fiancé, Frank."

She watched Rosalyn's face turn pale, then flush almost purple.

But the young woman quickly recovered her poise. "I could wish he *were,*" Rosalyn said, her eyes sliding greedily over him.

The pause that ensued was the kind often described as pregnant.

"I understand," Frank said, "that you told my sister that you and I were engaged. I'd like an explanation."

"Well, dear heart, it's plain you don't remember we met in Tokyo and—"

"I remember meeting some girl there. Yes, it might have been you. The girl made very little impression, so it could easily have been you."

Rosalyn flushed angrily. "You got drunk and asked me to marry you."

"I never get drunk, and I don't believe I exchanged more than three words with you, if that. Now I'm still waiting for an explanation."

Rosalyn's eyes darkened threateningly and she looked away from him. Then her laugh pealed musically. "Oh, you're wonderful! You're the funniest man in the world!"

"Yeah. I knock myself out. I'm a scream, all right!"

Lexi had had enough. "I gather that Rosalyn was exaggerating when calling herself your fiancée," she said tightly.

"You gather correctly," Frank said.

"I always knew the letter introducing her to me supposedly written by you was a fake."

"And that's a misdemeanor," Frank said. "Punishable by a certain fine and a period in jail. I don't remember, Lexi. Is there a police force in Lookaway?"

"You're not going to do anything." Rosalyn's voice was an octave higher than her usual soft purr. "I'll tell the authorities about your smuggled gold and jewels! I'll tell them about their hiding place, I'll show them the closet and help them break down the door!"

"Come here, Rosalyn," Lexi said. "Let me show you something."

She led the reluctant young woman into the back room and opened the closet.

"Someone has taken them, Rosalyn. And if it wasn't you, then who was it? Who's in cahoots with you?"

Rosalyn's startled surprise seemed proof that she was innocent of the theft. Her consternation was evident and the distress on her pretty face quite plain.

"I don't know," she wailed. "One of those paintings is *mine!* The cat. The cat is mine! I have to get it back! I *have* to!"

"Why do you think the cat is yours?" Lexi asked.

"I—I was told to ingratiate myself with you and—and pick up the painting of the cat. Buy it, if possible, but get it one way or another."

"Who told you?" Frank asked.

"I don't know, but I was to be rewarded with thousands of dollars. Oh, what will I do? What can I do?" Rosalyn turned on Lexi. "You!" she shouted. "With your artlessness, your sweetness and naivete, keeping me out of the gallery, making me stay at the inn! It's *your* fault. You tricked me!"

"I think you'd better go," Frank said to the angry young woman, "and I believe you'd be wise not to return." He looked at his sister. "Don't you agree, Lexi?" he asked. "Or do you want to question her? She's liable to go into a towering rage or a cardiac arrest any minute."

Trembling with anger and frustration, Rosalyn stormed out of the gallery.

"What a witch!" Frank said. "Could you really believe she was my fiancée?"

"It wasn't easy."

"Let's finish what we started, Lexi. Let's look in your trash."

They went out and around the building. A cat, probably the same creature who'd disturbed Lexi one night with its foraging, was sunning itself on top of the trash lid. It opened one citrine eye at the intruders before stretching and loping off.

The trash can was empty.

"Never mind, Lex. It wouldn't have told us much, anyway. Now this man you started to tell me about who was looking for illegal valuables. Who is he? I want to meet him."

"He's Keith Hamilton and he's staying at the inn. But, Frank, there's another man who's interested in the smuggled jewels. His name is Jeff Warner. Hadn't I better describe the paintings to you?"

Oh, the relief of having Frank to lean on!

"Of course."

"There's a very pink poodle, bulbous. I mean the paint is put on so thick it's like chunks of bubble gum. And I think the paint is covering stuff that's valuable. And then there's a big cat with pasted-on plastic eyes, but Keith said they were opals. It has a necklace that must be made of diamonds or something. There's a temple whose frame sent Jeff into spasms and there's an abstract. I don't have any idea about what the abstract is hiding. And now we may never know! Frank, one of the three, either Rosalyn, Jeff, or Keith stole the paintings. I thought I heard something the night before last, but I think I already told you that."

"Those four paintings—were the artists' names familiar to you?"

"I didn't even look. I wouldn't even call them art. They were terrible! The most incompetent work I've ever seen!"

"Well," Frank said, "I've certainly come back to the States to find things aren't dull here. Come on, lock the gallery and let's go to the inn."

When they arrived at the inn, Lexi saw Keith and three other men coming up from the eighteenth green. A yearning ache swelled within her as he neared her. She longed to touch him, to hold his hand.

"Well, hello!" he said. "I'm glad to see you, Lexi."

"This is my brother, Frank," Lexi said and watched the men shake hands. "We— we want to ask you some questions, Keith."

"Okay. Will you join me in a beer? Golf is hot work on a day like this. Oh-oh, what's Rosalyn in a huff about?"

He directed their attention to the glamorous woman, who was stalking toward the practice tee and viciously whirling a golf club as she went.

"She's not all sweetness and light today, is she?" Keith said.

"We had a flaming row," Lexi said.

Just then Bob came up. "Good morning to you all," he said. "I do believe this gentleman must be your brother, Lexi. There is a distinct resemblance."

"Yes, this is Frank. I thought you'd met each other before. But I guess you were always busy when Frank visited me. Frank, this is Bob Pierce, the owner-manager of the inn and a good friend of mine."

"Hey!" Jeff came running up. "A party, is it?"

"No, Jeff, not a party. A—a meeting, sort of," Lexi said.

"Ah, well, man cannot live by caviar alone. I'd like to try, though."

"Jeff is the third party involved whom I told you about, Frank," Lexi said. "He might as well be questioned, too, don't you think?"

"Sounds like a private consultation," Bob said, "so if you'll excuse me..." He left.

Soon the three young men and Lexi were sitting on an empty part of the inn's wide veranda. They looked uncomfortably at each other.

To break the silence, Frank said, "I can't stand limp handshakes. They repel me."

Lexi didn't know whose handshake he was referring to.

She said, "Jeff, in case you haven't guessed, this is my brother. We came to tell you and Keith that the closet in my back room has been burgled. The paintings have gone!"

"The poodle? My dog has been stolen?" Jeff's voice was harsh with shock.

Keith's sleepy eyes were suddenly wide awake.

"Lexi, do you know who it was or when it took place?"

"No. Frank wants to ask you about the paintings. I'd assumed they were sent by him, but he knows nothing about them. Tell him, please, what you told us."

Keith looked from one to the other, then said, "I am here to trace smuggled and stolen jewels and gold. The Customs people, the Treasury Department, and the F.B.I. are all concerned. A certain amount of stolen goods has been traced to Lookaway Mountain. There are more smuggled treasures going to other art galleries and boutiques around the nation, but this place is my concern at present."

Lexi had her eyes on Jeff while Keith told them his role in the search. Jeff was looking sick.

Keith continued. "The poodle Jeff is so

interested in would be a fine example of how the stuff is concealed when and if we find it. Just what is your interest, Jeff? Are you a part of the smuggling ring? No, don't answer. Not now. Now as to the poodle. One look at it and I knew. Gold coins are coated in wax to protect them from the acrylic, then are placed on the muscular parts of the subject and painted over, thickly. An art enthusiast can know a bad painting, but it takes experience to know exactly where to look for the loot. The painting of the cat is a good example of camouflage. The opal eyes would be valued at several thousand dollars each. The necklace is made of uncut diamonds—at goodness knows how much apiece. Which reminds me, why isn't Rosalyn in on this conference?"

"Rosalyn is a fake and a liar, but I'm quite sure she didn't steal the paintings," Lexi said. "She couldn't have faked her surprise and distress when she saw the empty closet. It has to be either you, Keith, or you, Jeff, who stole them. That's why Frank and I are here. To learn the truth."

Chapter Nine

"*I* certainly didn't steal the darn things," Jeff said sulkily. "If I had, I'd have been long gone from Lookaway Mountain, I can tell you! I'd have taken that poodle to New York and—and—"

"Why are you here, Jeff?" Lexi asked. "What made you come to my gallery and ask for a dog painting? How did you know about the smuggled gold and stuff?"

There was dead silence as Jeff seemed to be making up his mind just how to answer her question. Both Keith and Frank were staring at him with unfriendly eyes.

"It was Rosalyn," Jeff finally said.

"What about Rosalyn?" Lexi demanded.

"I was given a message to contact an auburn-haired woman named Rosalyn Gray in Lookaway Mountain. After I had bought a poodle at your gallery, I was to tell her and she'd give me instructions."

"Who told you to do that?" Keith asked.

"Well, that's the funny part of it. I don't know who. I've talked to Rosalyn and she doesn't know either, or so she says."

"Better start from the beginning, Warner," Keith said. "Where were you when you got the message? How was the message given and, most important, why are you involved? Are you a thief?"

"Certainly not!" Jeff drew himself up to his full six feet. "I'm a private investigator. I wasn't too successful in New York when a marvelous opportunity to make a lot of money came my way. It wasn't, or so it seemed, anything illegal. I was told that gold and jewels that belonged to a defunct syndicate in the Orient were being shipped here and would belong to anybody just for the taking. I'd have to share, of course, with my unknown benefactor. To answer your question, the other one, it was a man's voice on the telephone that gave the message. It sounded too good to be true. It *was* too good to be true, and now I wish I was back home with my poor little private-eye business."

Frank got up. "I think we'd better get Rosalyn, don't you? There are too many unanswered questions. I'll get her." He hurried off.

Lexi turned to Keith. The smile on her face felt stitched on and her eyes were bright with anger.

"One of you three took the paintings," she said to him and turned to Jeff. "One of you is a liar. For a while Rosalyn had me convinced she was innocent of the theft, but now I believe she's such a consummate actress she has to be just as suspect as you two. Oh, here she comes."

Rosalyn was looking up at Frank's impassive face and being charming. When they reached the others and sat down, Rosalyn seemed to think she had fluttered her eyelashes enough. They were not having the desired result.

"Keith is a government investigator," Frank said. "Jeff is a private eye. What are *you*, Rosalyn?"

"Just a poor working girl!" she cooed.

"Nuts!" Lexi said impolitely.

"What were you doing in Tokyo where you said we got engaged?" Frank demanded.

Rosalyn looked uneasy. "I—I was sent there."

"To do what?"

"To find out when some paintings were to be sent here."

"Who sent you?"

"I don't know. He, whoever he was, said I could get thousands of dollars by simply buying a painting of a cat in Lookaway Mountain and bringing it to him."

"Aha! Where were you to bring it? We're getting somewhere now!" Frank said.

"I was to stay at Lookaway Mountain and he'd be in touch."

"Where did you get the idea to say you were my fiancée?"

"He told me to worm my way in. I'd found out that you, Frank, were the brother of the girl who owned the gallery where I'd get the cat. It seemed a simple task to introduce myself as a future sister-in-law—since I knew you'd be away—and to buy the exact painting I was supposed to. Alexis wouldn't let me stay, though, and I never had time to search for the painting."

"Why couldn't you have bought the painting in Tokyo if that's where it was?" Lexi asked.

"I'd have to declare it to customs or there might have been a search and I'd be arrested for smuggling."

"Do you know where the paintings are now, Rosalyn? Do you know who has them? Or who took them? Did *you?*" Keith asked the perspiring woman.

"I did not!"

"So here we have two persons who had reasons to steal and both deny it," Keith said.

"Three!" Frank corrected. "There have been unscrupulous government agents, you know. You, Keith, are not in the clear. Not one bit!"

"Well, neither are you, Frank! You say you didn't send the paintings and you seem to have arrived after they were sto-len, but what if you came a day or two earlier and hid somewhere? We're *all* of us suspects."

"Me, too?" Lexi asked. "I suppose I could have hidden them until the coast was clear and then—but I *didn't!* I *wouldn't!*" She took a deep breath. "And now what are we going to do? The inn will be closing after this weekend, not to open again un-til spring. Where will you all stay and how do we resolve all this? I'm sorry I can't put you up in my apartment. There's not enough room for even my brother."

"We'll find someplace. Not to worry about that, anyway," Frank said. "There's a boardinghouse, I seem to remember, be-hind the fire station. Is it still there?"

"Yes, but it's awfully run down," Lexi said.

"Look, Lex, I have to make a quick trip to New York," Frank said. "I'll be back the middle of the week."

"I have to go back to Greensboro," Keith said, "but only for a few days or so."

"I'd almost think you were all running away," Lexi said. "Jeff, are you staying?"

"Certainly am."

"Well, you can help me see that Keith doesn't depart with an overload of packages. Rosalyn, are you staying, too?"

"I'm not leaving without my cat!"

"Let's all walk over to the old boardinghouse then and give them warning you'll take up residence on Monday, shall we?" Lexi suggested.

As they were getting to their feet, Bob Pierce ambled up.

"Just wanted to tell you about closing the inn for the winter. Doesn't feel like winter now, does it? But sudden storms come up. I like the place to be all battened down before I leave for Atlanta."

"Where do you stay while the inn's being closed?" Lexi asked Bob.

"I make do with Mrs. Harris's boardinghouse. It's pretty bad, but it's clean."

"Is Mrs. Harris the wife of our general-store man?"

"Yes, why?"

"No reason. But I think Mrs. Harris will have an influx of boarders, then. That's where we're going now."

"Oh, I wouldn't advise it," Bob said.

"You won't like it, you know."

"I'm afraid that there's unfinished business that will keep us here for a while," Jeff said.

"Er—Lexi," Bob began, "I'd like some advice from you. My sister just sent me a set of acrylics. She wants me to be an artist. But the tubes are solid. How do you soften acrylics?"

"You don't, Bob. Once hardened, they stay hardened. Sorry. Get yourself some oils."

They left Bob leaning on the railing of the veranda and walked off.

When they got to the gallery, Lexi opted against opening it up for the present. She wanted to see what Mrs. Harris's place was like.

As they went past the fire house, Lexi told them of the elaborate fire-alarm system Bob had installed in the inn.

"The inn is old, you know, although Bob hasn't owned it more than a few years, and it's made of wood. So every room has a smoke detector that signals the fire house directly. His insurance has been greatly reduced because of it. Well, here's the boarding house. What do you think of it?"

Rosalyn groaned. "I hate roughing it," she said. "If I have to share a bathroom, I think I'll scream."

"Maybe the paintings will be found and the mystery mastermind revealed before Monday," Keith said. "Whoever managed this get-rich-quick scheme should be severely punished."

They trooped up five worn steps to a sagging porch and rang the bell.

Rosalyn hung back, whispering to Lexi, "I'll give you half my share of the cat if *you'll* stay here and let me use your apartment."

Lexi shook her head. "Sorry."

The door was opened by a gray-haired woman who looked astonished when Jeff said they'd like to see her rooms.

"How many?" the woman asked. *"All* of you?"

"Three of us starting Monday and a fourth coming midweek."

"The men will have to double up," Mrs. Harris said. "My best room is reserved for

Mr. Pierce from the inn, but I've got a couple more."

"Have you any with a private bath?" Rosalyn asked.

"There's one bathroom on the second floor and another on the third. None private."

Lexi left them to talk room and board and went back to her gallery. She wouldn't see Frank again until he returned from New York. He planned on catching the bus to Asheville, then flying. She wondered if Keith would be taking the same bus. She'd like to see him alone, talk to him, look at him.

She bypassed the gallery and climbed the stairs to her apartment. No matter what happened or how lonely she became, she had her apartment.

Each morning she could admire her color scheme, her paintings, smiling, happy, and reassured. It was her sanctuary, her own nest. She could put fear in another compartment of her mind and forget her troubles.

She thought about Keith again as she

sat in front of her picture window. She wished he were here. She pictured his eyes, those cold gray eyes that sometimes warmed up as he looked at her. They were the color of rain on a clean window. She hugged herself.

She thought of Bob's hardened acrylics and wondered how his sister could have made such a mistake if she knew anything about paints. She thought of the inn, its homelike atmosphere, and was thankful it was so close to her gallery.

Lexi thought of everything but the one subject she wanted to avoid. At last it thrust itself at her and she faced it.

Both Jeff and Rosalyn had been sent here to Lookaway Mountain, to her gallery, in search of what they were supposed to acquire in the pursuit of riches. Why her gallery? Because there was someone, the mystery mastermind, as Keith called him, who was familiar with this town, knew about her gallery, and thought she'd be a pushover when his minions tried to buy. It would seem he knew her, and so she must know *him!* Who?

And why had Keith come, straight as

a homing pigeon, to question her?

Oh, she hated unsolved puzzles, hated mysteries, hated feelings of uncertainty. If only this whole mess were cleared up.

A knock on her door interrupted her thoughts. Lexi ran to open it and her heart flipped over when she saw Keith standing there.

As he entered, he told her, "Lexi, I must say your apartment is about the freshest, prettiest, coziest I've ever had the pleasure of seeing. And you—you're the freshest, prettiest, sweetest girl that ever drew breath. Lexi." He paused, then drew her close and kissed the hollow of her throat.

Suddenly, their lips met and Lexi's ecstasy was almost unbearable.

"I have to leave in a minute," he said, pushing her gently away from him. "We haven't got time to kid around."

"W-were we kidding?" Lexi's voice was small.

"No, no, that's not what I meant. Now I want you to be extra careful about letting people in your home. You let *me* in and you shouldn't have. Now when this mess is all cleared up, I'll be going off on other assignments, you know."

"Will I ever see you again when it's all over?" Lexi asked.

"Of course, you will."

"You mean once a year with bewildering frequency, huh?" She got a case of hiccups and turned away.

"I can't commit myself yet, Lexi, but I can tell you it will be considerably oftener. Goodby, I'll probably be back by Monday." He left without a further kiss or a word of love.

Chapter Ten

"Someone we know stole the paintings," Jeff said. "It has to be a person who knows your gallery, Lexi, and who knows the inn, the locale, and so forth. Now who could it be?"

Jeff had come into the gallery after lunch. He went on. "And let's say we find them stashed away someplace. What happens? Does Rosalyn get her cat? Do I get my poodle? I think we're wasting time. That Rosalyn, that wide-eyed dewy innocence! I'd trust her as far as I could throw a piano!"

137

Lexi sighed. "I believe that before the inn closes, I'll search Rosalyn's room, *your* room, too, and Keith's. That will make me feel as though I'm doing something constructive. The paintings can't have evaporated."

"I've already searched Keith's and Rosalyn's rooms. I don't have to search mine because I know I haven't got them. Perhaps we should search every room in the inn. Will Bob Pierce let us?"

"I'm not sure he will if there are still some guests around. He wouldn't let us disturb *them,* you know."

"The inn is quite empty," Jeff said. "I think there are no more than a dozen people lingering till the last minute. The tapes on the tennis courts have been removed, the pro shop is locked up, and the dining room is serving only buffet style. It's pretty dismal now and I, for one, won't mind moving to the boardinghouse. Shall we go together to ask Bob's permission to search?"

"Well, all right. Business at this gallery is less than thriving at present, so I won't miss much by leaving."

They walked companionably toward the inn, chatting a little and not minding the comfortable silences in between.

"Treasure," Jeff said, "is elusive, a will-o'-the-wisp that has a way of not being where it's supposed to be."

"I'm sure you're right. I don't at all look forward to starting a room-to-room scouring of the inn. It's an event that I can't contemplate with any enthusiasm. I don't like asking Bob's permission either. He doesn't know what we're looking for or why it's important to find the paintings. He will think we're mad or having an attack of the whimsy. Ah, there's Rosalyn on the veranda."

Rosalyn was the center of a small group. She was very animated and chatty, posing her face this way and that, as if a camera were aimed at her. There were suitcases and tote bags waiting to be put into cars, and soon there came a flurry of goodbys as two people left and another three prepared to leave.

Bob Pierce hurried up to shake the departing guests' hands. Before he rushed back inside, Lexi approached him.

"Bob, this may sound silly, but there are some paintings missing from my gallery. Can Jeff and I look through your vacant rooms? The inn is a place where they might be hidden."

Bob looked at her in astonishment. "Are you saying that a guest of the inn has stolen—"

"No, Bob, I don't mean that, exactly. Someone, not necessarily one of your guests, has—oh, what's the use? I can't explain. May we search the rooms or not?"

"I'm afraid not, Lexi. They are automatically searched as they're cleaned and locked up. I'm sorry. There are only a few occupied right now, and I can't let you disturb the occupants. Now I've got to go. There's so much to do!" He hurried off.

Rosalyn came up to them. "This place is like a mausoleum," she declared. "I can't wait to leave. Even to a place like Mrs. Harris's. I may go there early."

"Rosalyn," Lexi said, "can we look for the paintings in your room? Now I'm not accusing you! Someone might have planted them, you know. Can we search?"

Rosalyn's eyes had changed to narrow slits of topaz steel and her lips lifted away from her mouth. The expression lasted only a few seconds and then she was her usual self again.

"Why, of course," she said sweetly. "But why don't you split up? You don't have to search together, do you? Why not separate and take in more territory? Jeff, I'll take you to my room." She looked arch as she invited him.

Lexi was left alone. It was all right with her. She had remembered some storage rooms hidden behind the pro shop where Bob had let her keep her furniture when she was about to move into her apartment a few years ago. She hoped she recalled the exact place. There was a row of small rooms, some used to store extra bits of furniture, some used for sports gear, and so forth. Surely Bob wouldn't mind if she looked there. Well, she wouldn't tell him.

She walked toward the pro shop—casually, as if she had no destination but was enjoying the Indian summer.

And there it was, the place she had in

mind. She opened the first door and peered in. At first the room looked quite bare, but there was a pile of something in one corner and a rolled-up awning in another. She went in.

The room was square, not very big, one small barred window high in the wall and the usual smoke detector on the ceiling.

She first went to the pile. Disappointed, she found it consisted of old, discarded menus from the dining room. She turned her attention to the awning. It was while she was poking through its folds, and sneezing a bit from its dust, that she heard the door close.

It took Lexi a full ten seconds to realize what had happened. The knob was missing from the handle on her side of the door. She was trapped, and suddenly she knew it was no accident. A dreadful feeling of terror overcame her.

The person who had pelted her with golf balls, the one who had locked her in the back-room closet, who had whispered in the forest, and who undoubtedly had examined her trash, was now responsible for the closed door.

She pushed her shoulder against the thick wood until it hurt. Then Lexi banged on it with a shoe, calling for help and trying not to get too panicky.

Well, she told herself, someone would come by. She'd hear him and calmly ask to be set free. In the meantime, she would examine the old menus again. There was something she remembered, something that niggled at her mind. something in the pile that she should have looked at more carefully before.

Now she lifted one menu at a time until she came to the thing—a cardboard that looked to be the backing of a picture, and in one corner there was a fragment of purple-and-green canvas. The abstract painting had been purple and green, hadn't it? Did that mean somebody had brought the paintings here? Did it mean that the abstract had been taken apart for its concealed treasure?

Frantically now, Lexi made a search of the floor, the corners, the baseboards. There was a tiny, shiny scrap of pink wedged under the doorsill. Was the pink a part of the lumpy poodle? She thought it was. She had been right in believing the paintings might have been hidden in this small room, but, of course, they were no longer here.

She kept on searching, however, combing the rough floorboards and running fingers on splintery rafters. The light had become dim. It was late afternoon and the small window made only a ghostly square of cobwebby gray.

It was no use to look anymore. Lexi wished that Keith had not left for Greensboro. She wished that Frank had not gone to New York. There was Jeff, but he probably would think she'd gone home and so would Rosalyn. Bob—if only he'd come down this way to see that all was locked up—but he was busy inside the inn.

Once again Lexi hammered on the door. Was there a noise outside? Had she heard someone? She called and listened, called and listened. It almost seemed that there was a quiet laugh just outside her door, but she must be mistaken. The wind sometimes sounded like something human.

It was getting cold. The warmth of the day was completely gone. Lexi shivered.

She stamped her feet and moved about. Would this ordeal never end?

Time moved erratically. Lexi had to concentrate to sense its passage. The beating of her heart, her own measured breathing, a cramping muscle were her clocks. Her mind strayed and the clocks stopped, then started again.

And now she knew she wouldn't be rescued until tomorrow—if then. There was a great void inside her. Instead of fright, there was acceptance. Instead of anger, there was apathy. There were three likely people who could have shut her away. There was Rosalyn, there was Jeff, and there was Bob. But if it were Bob, it had to have been an accident.

Soon moonlight flooded the small window, bathing the rough walls with a cold silver. Lexi shivered and tried to wrap herself up in the stiff awning. Suddenly, an idea came to her. She would get help quickly now.

She always had a packet of matches

with her, not because she smoked cigarettes, but because often she had to heat up a screw cap on a tube of paint before it could be opened.

She made an elongated roll of menus and set the end of it on fire. Standing on the folded awning, she held up her torch as far as she could reach toward the smoke detector.

The torch was smoking dreadfully and burning too quickly. It burned her fingers. She made herself another torch and then another, coughing as she did so, her eyes inflamed and weeping.

"Oh, please!" she prayed to the detector. *"Do* something!"

And suddenly she heard the screech of an alarm. It went on and on, but nobody came to investigate. Nobody cared that she had inhaled a dangerous amount of smoke. Evidently, nobody knew where the smoke was coming from.

The whole pile of menus had caught on fire from sparks and was smoldering. The canvas awning was Lexi's only hope of not smothering to death. She made herself a dusty cave of it and passed out.

She didn't hear the fire engines coming close nor the shouts nor the splash of water as hoses were trained on the storage room. She didn't hear the anguished cries of her rescuers.

She woke up in a hospital in Highlands. Her lungs felt parched and shriveled. Her throat was raw. Her eyes hurt. One hand was bandaged. And she felt all alone and lonely.

There was a knock on her white door and someone familiar called her name.

"Keith?" she said in a strange voice, a little old lady's voice. "Oh, Keith!"

She was out of the hospital by the time Frank returned. It was decided that for her safety she must stay in Mrs. Harris's boardinghouse with the others—at least until her health was back to normal and certain other things had been cleared up. Mrs. Harris was flustered, but with the help of the food from her husband's store, the meals were exceptionally good.

Lexi told only her brother about being deliberately locked in the inn's storage room. The others thought it an unfortunate accident. She told Frank about finding a shred of purple and green canvas on a discarded cardboard, and also a tiny scrap of pink that could have come from the poodle. Frank had never seen the stolen paintings and so could make no judgment, but he looked wise and gave her the annoying "pretty-girl-shouldn't-bother-her-little-head" bit, saying that he'd do the worrying from here on out.

It worried Lexi that she didn't feel confident enough about Keith to have told him all she confided to Frank. She loved Keith—she knew that—but that didn't mean he was innocent. He might have lied about going to Greensboro. Or he might have sneaked back to town.

Bob Pierce was not at his sunniest when faced with smoke damage and a ruined awning, but he rallied after scolding Lexi about poking into places where she didn't belong.

Mrs. Harris's boardinghouse had narrow halls, low-roofed and seamed with stains of age and dampness. It was anything but glamorous. However, Lexi had a comfortable feeling about being with the others. There was safety in numbers.

The weather was changing. A sterner season was claiming the earth. A steady northwest wind brought a high fog to the town. The fog dropped a thick veil between the boardinghouse and the other buildings. Although Lexi missed her lovely apartment, it was cozy to be in her opened-door room and hear the others talk.

She was sitting in a straight-backed chair in front of the narrow window adding up some figures from her gallery when Jeff came in without knocking.

Of course, her door was open so she couldn't feel too annoyed with him. She was amazed when he closed the door behind him.

"I think," he said harshly, "that Keith has gained some kind of hypnotic influence over you." Gone was his light tone, his joshing. "I tell you, you'd live to regret marrying him! That's if I let you!"

"What do you mean if you let me?"

"Precisely that I won't."

"I abhor precise people," Lexi said as

calmly as possible. "And you have nothing to say about it, anyway. Besides, he hasn't even proposed."

He gripped her wrist, forcing her to her feet and then pulling her to him, hurting her. She struggled, gasping.

His mouth was a slit and his eyes steely.

"You're hurting me, Jeff."

"I mean to. I've been Mr. Nice Guy long enough."

She cried out, but her throat hadn't healed enough for a cry to be more than a kitten-like mewling.

"Please," she whispered.

But he began to kiss her, and he was not gentle.

At that moment the door burst open and Keith came in, pulling Jeff away. Keith's eyes were as opaque as metal and his mouth was hard. His cheeks were drained by anger.

Everything happened too fast to seem real. Keith sent a bone-crunching blow to Jeff's face. Jeff staggered, spitting blood. He stood there, fists clenched, then lunged at Keith, but Keith's fist slammed into his jaw again. Jeff struck back, but Keith crouched like a leopard. Jeff wasn't able to touch him when Keith came after him again. Jeff tried to hit back, but his timing was off.

There was applause from the doorway. Rosalyn stood there clapping her hands and laughing.

Jeff's face was bloody and his eyes were swollen almost shut. He leaned groggily against the wall, no longer putting up a defense. He slowly slipped to the floor.

Keith went over to him, helped him to his feet, and slowly maneuvered him out the door and across the hall into the room they shared.

Rosalyn left, too, chuckling softly.

Chapter Eleven

Lexi was shaken. Jeff's rough kiss was unexpected and unwelcome. And then the fight between the two men had been a shattering thing to watch. Where was Frank when she needed him? Where was Bob? Where was Mrs. Harris?

Her lips were dry, her cheeks hot. She tried to rally her flagging spirits by assuring herself that not *every* girl had a couple of attractive men fighting over her. But were they *really* fighting over her? Or were they just fighting?

"Miss Steele?" Mrs. Harris called from downstairs. "Someone to see you!"

152

Lexi quickly ran a comb through her hair and hurried down the squeaking stairs. There, at the bottom, stood the old couple who had been on the picnic with them. What was their name? Terry, yes, that's what it was.

They greeted each other politely and then Mr. Terry said, "Will you take a short walk with us? As you see, we're still here. Rented a private cottage for another month. The weather isn't pleasant, but we'd like to be able to talk in private."

"All right," Lexi said. "I'd really like to get out in some fresh air. Just wait a minute till I get my coat."

They walked toward the inn. The evenings were getting much shorter, Lexi noted, and there was a tang of frost in the air. The water of the lake had lost its deep azure blue and had faded to a color that was steely and cold in this late afternoon.

Mrs. Terry broke the silence that had lasted during the first part of the walk.

"My dear," she said, "you probably didn't know it, but you made a very favorable impression on me and my husband that day of the picnic."

"Why, thank you," Lexi said in surprise.

"What we want to do is to buy the inn, and if we could do that, we'd keep it open all year. I believe there's skiing nearby in the winter, isn't there?"

"Yes, there is. Often the ski runs have to have man-made snow on them. It all depends on the weather. But, Mrs. Terry, I'm sure, very sure, that Bob Pierce doesn't want to sell, doesn't even *think* of selling out."

Mr. Terry spoke. "Pierce has not done very well with the inn, I'm sorry to say. His debts are great. But that's beside the point. If, and I say *if*, we can buy it, we'd like you to be hostess for us. You have a way about you that people like."

Lexi was stunned. "Me? But I've never been very popular. I—I'd like to think I have a way about me, but I'm terribly afraid I'm not very good with people. Anyway, I have my art gallery to run."

"Do show us your gallery, dear," Mrs. Terry said. She nudged her husband as if to say, "Don't push her."

"I'd love to," Lexi said. "It's that small house down the street."

"Is it successful?" Mr. Terry asked.

"Oh, very!" said Lexi quickly. Then she added, "Well, not really what you'd call terribly prosperous, but I love anything that has to do with art. And I even sold a painting of my own."

"This is an attractive little house," Mrs. Terry said.

"I'm afraid it may be cold and damp inside right now. I usually live upstairs, but I'm staying with my brother in the boardinghouse for a few days."

She unlocked the gallery door.

"Lovely!" Mrs. Terry exclaimed. "Beautifully displayed. You could keep this going while being a hostess, you know. You could even live upstairs part of the time if you wanted."

"Mrs. Terry, I do appreciate your offer, but I'm quite sure Bob won't give up the inn. Anyway, I—I might get married. That is, I'm not engaged or anything, but I'm the right age to think about marriage. I'm the right age to think about having a family. I mean, I'm the right age to hope!"

"Of course, you are," Mrs. Terry said comfortingly. "And you're certainly attractive enough. Well, dear, we won't push you for an answer. Everything hinges on Mr. Pierce being willing to sell. Just keep your options open, will you? Oh, what a lovely painting of wildflowers! I've simply *got* to have it for my morning room! Is it very expensive?"

"Rather a lot," Lexi said, "but it's worth every cent."

"So nice to see a *good* painting," Mrs. Terry went on. "We saw a horrid one at the inn. It was supposed to be leaning, face in, against a wall in an upstairs hall but had fallen. It was really terrible!"

Lexi had immediately pricked up her ears.

"What was it like?" she asked eagerly.

"It was one of those modern monstrosities, all purple and green. Now tell me the price of the wildflowers."

Lexi quoted the price and was happy to see that it had not discouraged the elderly lady.

Lexi questioned her further. "Who did this painting—this purple monstrosity—belong to, do you know?"

"No. When we passed the same place later, it was gone. Will you accept a check, dear? Good! I'm so happy with my new painting and I will be equally happy when you are our hostess if and when we acquire the inn. Thank you for walking along with us. We'll leave you now."

Lexi took time to put another painting in the vacant space left by the sold picture and then she dusted a bit and threw out the trash.

She locked up, then climbed her outside stairs to the apartment. As usual, the colors, the furnishings, and the quiet beauty of it gave Lexi great pleasure. She dusted a little before sitting in her favorite chair by the picture window.

How would she like to be hostess for the inn? It would be nice. That was, if her hopes were unfulfilled. What hopes? Hopes of a life with Keith even though she was unsure of his integrity? She meditated and watched the end of day reflected on Stone Mountain.

She must get back to the boardinghouse. It would be fine if she could resolve her problems before returning to the others.

Sundown was what she was waiting for, but the sun lingered on top of the mountain as if it were glued there. Its descent was so slow it reminded her of the hands on a watch. As she watched and waited, someone knocked on her door.

Suddenly, she was frightened. It was a fear that numbed her senses.

"Wh—who's there?" Her voice quavered.

"It's me, Keith. You shouldn't be all alone, you *know* that, Lexi!"

Lexi opened the door, but she was still alarmed. What guarantee did she have that Keith was not her enemy? But when he entered, her heart gave a leap of joy and she lifted her face to a hoped-for kiss.

"Hmm," Keith said. "You are conceited! I have no intention of kissing someone who has so little faith! You have not trusted me for a long time. And yet you expect affection from me!"

Lexi opened her mouth but could not think of anything horrid to say. She just glared at him.

"That's better," Keith said. "And you know very well that you shouldn't have opened the door to me. Especially if you're still in a quandary about me and my integrity. Silly girl—silly, lovely, adorable girl!"

He sat down on one end of the sofa.

"Now tell me why you're here, Lexi. Why aren't you in the boardinghouse where we can keep an eye on you?"

Lexi, still scowling, fire in her eyes, said, "It's none of your business what I do or why I do it!"

Keith got up to close the gap between them. He took her by the shoulders and shook her gently. It seemed quite natural then that his arms should find themselves around her slender body and that his lips should seek hers.

Lexi tried not to respond, but the kiss was so sweet, his arms so strong. She couldn't help kissing him back. Then she pushed away from him. She wished to stay angry.

Keith resumed his seat with a salute.

"I'm waiting for you to tell me," he said.

There was no reason to keep the Terrys'

offer a secret. As a matter of fact, it would do Keith good to realize that she had a pleasant future in store for her if she wanted it. One that had no dependence on him or his plans. She told him.

Keith was thoughtful. "Is this something you'd really like, Lexi? Are you sure of your fondness for people? Are you so fond of them you could stand to be at their beck and call constantly? Would you like matrons complaining about Bingo calls being too fast? Or old gentlemen, under the guise of fatherliness, squeezing you, planting kisses on your brow and flirting? Would you like to organize bridge contests, putting contests, and masquerade balls?"

"Heavens!" Lexi exclaimed. "You seem to know a lot about being a hostess!" A laugh forced itself through her firmly compressed lips and her face relaxed into its usual captivating mien.

"There you go, darling," Keith said. "Your pretty face looks much better when you're not cross."

"I have a lot to be cross about," Lexi

said, trying unsuccessfully to put on another scowl. "I have worries you don't even know about."

"Tell me about them."

"No, but I'll tell you *one* important fact. The Terrys saw the purple-and-green abstract in one of the inn's halls. They just happened to tell me because they bought a lovely painting from me and compared it to the hideous one they'd seen by mistake at the inn. Of course, when they passed by again, the abstract was gone. But, Keith, you see, don't you, that I was correct in believing the paintings are hidden somewhere in the inn? I'll tell you something else. I was *locked* inside the inn's storage room. It was no accident."

"I know that, Lexi. Frank told me. He told me also that I'm one of the people you suspect of locking you in. I swear I'm not. And while I'm at it, I wish to commend you on getting the smoke detector working. It was a smart move. Next time, though, don't let other things catch on fire. You are lucky, darling, that you were rescued before the smoke inhalation did permanent harm. Well, let me walk you back to the boardinghouse. It's getting late."

Keith helped Lexi lock up and they strolled, hand in hand, up the road toward Mrs. Harris's.

The evening sky had rid itself of the clouds that had marred it all day and now it was star-studded.

The first to greet them at the door was Rosalyn. She attempted to look roguish as she chided them about being lovers in the gloaming, but Lexi could see that bitterness lurked beneath her playful tone. Lexi had a fleeting sympathy for the young woman. If their positions had been reversed—Rosalyn holding hands with Keith—she wasn't sure she could hide her feelings as well as Rosalyn did.

Jeff came up. "I'd like a word with you, Lexi," he said. "And to *you,* Keith, all I can say is the better man won. Sorry about being such a donkey."

Keith smiled at Jeff's halfhearted apology and watched Lexi and Jeff go up the stairs together. Frank pulled Keith aside for a few private words and Rosalyn wandered off toward the dining room.

At the head of the stairs and just outside Lexi's room Jeff took her hand.

"I'm dreadfully sorry about what happened. I don't know what got into me. It might have been a combination of having you like Keith better than me and the frustration of having lost the painting and what it would have meant to my lean bank account. I wonder if you can forgive me."

"Of course, I'll forgive you, Jeff. We'll continue to be friends. You've given me laughs and lighthearted banter and I'll always think of you as a wonderful person."

"That's me all right. Beautiful girls think me wonderful but never, never romantic!" He sighed and Lexi laughed.

To everybody's surprise, Frank and Keith excused themselves from dinner, saying they had made plans to talk to someone somewhere and that they'd get something to eat later on.

Jeff kept the conversation going in his old inimitable fashion during dinner, but there was a lack of enthusiasm about lingering for coffee in the drawing room.

Good nights were said cordially. Everybody clearly wanted to be left alone to think, to calculate, to plan.

Lexi wanted the time to dream about Keith, to think about the Terrys' offer and to quell the constant fear that had almost become a part of her.

Chapter Twelve

The next evening Rosalyn excused herself very early, saying she was tired and was going to bed. Lexi, for some reason, believed Rosalyn's statement was covering up some secret plan. She waited and wondered and felt something was up. And she went up to her own room, keeping an ear open for Rosalyn's door.

But Rosalyn made no move till everyone had retired. Then Lexi heard soft footfalls going past her door. There was one step on the staircase that squeaked when trod upon and she listened for it. Then she heard it.

It was the signal for Lexi to follow and, with the caution of a thief, she made her way down the stairs and out into the dark.

Black clouds chased across a feeble moon and chill spurts of autumn made themselves felt at odd moments.

Rosalyn was a furtive figure as she went down the road hugging shadows, avoiding starlight, and hurrying in spurts when she was assured of nobody watching. Lexi followed a half block behind. She was equally careful not to be noticed.

Perhaps this was a wild-goose chase, but Lexi had a strong feeling that something important was about to happen. Rosalyn had been jumpy all day, peevish and irritable when anyone addressed her in conversation.

Jeff had been the recipient of most of her barbed remarks, but he had shrugged them off with a quip or two. He, for one, seemed back to his old witticisms—nothing bothered him, and he acted as if his conscience were spotless.

Keith had been somber. Rosalyn told everybody that Keith was as much fun as a graveyard.

Keith's rejoinder was that Rosalyn's mind was as shallow as a rain puddle.

Frank had been in a brown study all day. Occasionally he'd get a mysterious telephone call, and he'd talk only in monosyllables, so no one could get a glimmer of what the call was about.

Bob Pierce had spent most of the daylight hours at the inn, doing what innkeepers did to batten down for winter. Then, after dinner, he returned to the inn.

Tonight Frank and Keith had disappeared again on some mysterious errand.

Soon Lexi's eyes became accustomed to the dark and could pick out the deepening of a shadow or a movement of a bush. Rosalyn appeared and disappeared as she kept herself, she obviously hoped, screened from view.

Lexi had an uncertain moment of wondering if Rosalyn was going to meet someone she loved. Of course, that was her own private business.

Well, Lexi wouldn't expose anything that had to do with romance. But somehow Rosalyn did not look romantic.

Where was Rosalyn going? She had

passed Mr. Harris's store and passed Lexi's gallery and seemed to be heading for the lake. Or was she going to the back entrance of the inn?

Lexi fell behind a bit. There was open space ahead where she might be detected. She saw Rosalyn running now, crossing over the path, pushing between lilac bushes and then disappearing completely.

Lexi hurried toward the inn. The door to the big kitchen seemed to be the one Rosalyn was headed for. It was the closest. She'd have to circle the complete inn to get to the veranda and the main entrance.

Again Lexi wondered if she were on a screwball chase or whether the missing paintings would be found at last. Surely that was what Rosalyn was after. If it wasn't, then Lexi had miscalculated badly. Her misgivings were becoming worse now. Second thoughts made her want to turn around and go back to the safety of the boardinghouse.

What if suddenly Rosalyn and her boyfriend loomed up in front of her? What would she do? She would look and feel like an idiot!

All the same, Lexi went beyond the kitchen door. There was a window she could just barely see ahead of her that had a tiny slit of light pouring from it. To that window she proceeded on tiptoe.

She arrived at the window and affixed one eye to the slit of light. That's all it was big enough for. She saw a man's back. It was bent over a low table and seemed to be straining. She could hear nothing. The back must belong to Bob and she had a momentary yen to knock on the window to tell him that Rosalyn had entered his inn for some reason.

But Lexi wasn't sure that Rosalyn had really gone in, so she restrained herself. It was dull and uninteresting to stand among the bushes just to watch Bob with his eternal figuring. He was always looking at lists of figures. Although why his back showed strain was a question. She was about to turn away when suddenly Bob's back straightened and turned and she could see his face.

Could that face belong to Bob? Quiet, gentle Bob who was a friend to everyone? It was a face of hate and menace, of evil and malevolence. And it stared at an approaching figure. Lexi could see only a portion of the newcomer, but she knew it had to be Rosalyn.

Bob's facial expression hit Lexi a staggering blow. The thought that he could intend someone mischief had never occurred to her. But she could see that he was threatening Rosalyn. A long, sharp knife was in his hand.

What could he have been doing with such a knife as he pored over his accounts? Or wasn't it a ledger of figures at all but perhaps a painting to be taken apart?

This was the time to force her brain to work on every cylinder. Would it be better to pound on the window or would that precipitate the threatened violence? Would it be wise to retrace her steps and see if she could enter the building by the kitchen door?

Bob and Rosalyn seemed to be in sharp conversation now, angry, questioning, and tough. It would be best for Lexi to go through the kitchen and hope she'd find the lighted room before anything bad happened.

She discovered the door although the night was very dark now. She found it unlocked and slowly edged her way in. She tripped over a stool and then bumped into a table and stood still to listen. When nobody seemed to have heard her, she crept forward to where a dim light showed a door leading into a pantry.

Voices reached her now. Angry, threatening noises from Bob and frightened, pleading ones from Rosalyn.

Lexi followed the sounds. She surprised herself by feeling pity for Rosalyn. Rosalyn was obviously beyond her depth and *she,* Lexi, must get her out of a bad situation.

Light from under a door and louder voices made Lexi know she'd arrived at the scene.

She opened the door and stepped in.

Two pairs of eyes glued themselves to her. Two figures were frozen. Two pairs of lungs were inhaling and exhaling noisily.

"I—I thought I'd drop in," Lexi said. "I've come to take Rosalyn back with me."

Her words galvanized Bob. He leapt forward, grabbed her arm, and threw her into a corner. Then he threw Rosalyn on top of her. Not a word was spoken, but the atmosphere was thick with venom.

From somewhere Bob got hold of a length of cord, which he tested in his strong hands. The girls weren't passively waiting for his next move. They were almost on their feet when Bob pounced on them.

It was like having a nightmare come to life.

"Bob," Lexi said, "I'm sure you don't mean to hurt us." She tried to force a smile, but one side of her mouth decided to go numb. It was a feeble leer and she knew it probably made her look as frightened as she felt.

Bob quickly tied the two girls together, binding their hands behind them and roping them to an exposed pipe.

"Bob," Lexi tried again, "you're too nice a guy to—"

"Shut up!" Bob snarled. "The two of you

have ruined my plans. I hoped to continue to run the inn, but now, after I've gotten the jewels and coins out of the paintings, I'll have to burn the place and go away. I wish I could think of a suitable punishment for you, but I'll have to opt for setting the place on fire. This time they'll find two charred bodies. If only you hadn't been nosy!"

Lexi tried to ease her bound hands and wrists. The bright ember of hope turned to a cold lump of ash when she knew she couldn't talk him out of his plans.

Every adventure story she'd ever read had a heroine who fought through to the bitter end, made incredible escapes, and came through victorious. Why couldn't she?

Maybe Lexi could keep him talking. He was back at the table now and was trying to strip the canvas from the back of the poodle. He'd evidently found that the acrylic surface would not crack or break. Against the wall was the painting of the cat. It was blinded now. The opal eyes had been removed and the diamond necklace was gone. Beside it was the untouched

temple painting. Its frame had been removed. And there were shreds of purple
and green on the floor. He'd found *that*
treasure by tearing up the abstract. What
treasure was it, Lexi wondered, as if it
mattered!

"Bob." Lexi forced herself to speak
calmly. "Were you the one trying to hit
me with golf balls?"

Bob chuckled. "Sure was, honey. Almost got you, too! Gee, when you saw that
pile of wooden tees in the woods, I was
afraid you'd know it was me. I'm the only
one who has tees of that color."

"Were you the one who locked me in my
closet and searched the gallery?"

Bob nodded, busy with his knife. "Yep."

"And was it you who examined my
trash, whispered to me in the woods at
the picnic, locked me in your storage
room?"

"Yes. Now be quiet. This canvas is almost as hard as the acrylic. I want no
noise, no talk. I got to get the rest of the
gold out and leave."

"Why did you do all this? I thought we

were friends. How did you arrange to have the paintings sent to my gallery? How did you contact Rosalyn and Jeff? Is Keith in this racket, too, of smuggling jewels and gold? Why weren't you content to run a successful inn? Why?"

"Will you be quiet! Or will I have to tape your mouth?"

Lexi felt she must keep questioning, talking, disturbing him. She hoped he didn't have tape handy.

"How," she said, "did you get inside my gallery to steal the paintings?"

Bob gave a sort of snort. "Naturally, I have keys to all the cottages here at the inn. To all of the closets. And some of my keys fit your place. I didn't want the trouble of stealing, though. Rosalyn was supposed to buy the cat and Jeff was supposed to buy the poodle. Both were to be given to me. Later I'd have a couple of other people buy the temple and the abstract. But *you*, Lexi, you stubborn, hardheaded idiot, wouldn't sell. Ah," he sighed as he freed a gold coin from its nest of wax.

Lexi continued to pester him with questions. "When you told me your sister had sent you acrylic paints that had hardened, you were just trying to find out how to get the acrylic off the poodle, weren't you?"

Bob grunted.

"I imagine you have lots of girls," Lexi said, changing the subject abruptly.

"True," he said absently as he struggled to cut more of the canvas. "But I don't give a snap for any of them."

As Lexi talked, her hands were busy. She was still back to back with Rosalyn and her fingers tugged and tore at Rosalyn's rope. When finally the binding eased and Rosalyn could free her own hands, she did the same for Lexi.

It was harder to untie the knots on the pipe. They had to hold to their position, back to back, and work blindly. Any movement of their bodies could be seen by Bob who, although rapt in his exposure of gold coins, was halfway turned toward the two captives.

Rosalyn now took up the almost non-stop talk.

"Bob," she pleaded, tears in her voice, "you *can't* mean you're going to burn up the whole inn and us with it! You can't! You mustn't! Oh, please, Bob, we won't tell on you, we promise! And what good will it do you to lose the inn?"

"It's well insured. Too bad about you two girls. If you'd minded your own business and stayed at the boardinghouse— ah, another coin! This one is worth about five thousand dollars by itself!"

He bent over his work feverishly now, both hands moving, tearing and cutting the stiff canvas.

His absorption gave the girls their chance. Lexi's sore fingers finally shredded the cord's fibers and then it was easy to undo the knots.

She made a small gesture to Rosalyn, who seemed to get the message, and they quietly got to their feet and approached the concentrating scoundrel. With one concerted movement they attacked.

Lexi grabbed for the knife while Rosalyn gripped Bob's neck. His reaction was fast, and he almost threw off his assailants, but Lexi pointed the knife at his throat, almost pricking it, and he stopped struggling. Rosalyn held him tight.

"Now, girls," he said, "you know I was just joshing you! I wouldn't hurt a hair on your heads. Now put down the knife, dear, and—"

There was a clatter at the door, and Keith, Frank, and two unknown men crowded in, one of the unknowns displaying a gun.

It was soon over. Bob was handcuffed and led away. His cover was blown, his network of seven agents on the prowl for stolen gold and gems had been destroyed by Interpol.

It was decided that although all the jewels and gold and the platinum frame from the temple, as well as the folding money in back of the abstract, had to be returned to their owners, a reward to both Jeff and Rosalyn—who had not known they were dealing with stolen property—would be paid.

The rewards were not fortunes, but, as Jeff was quick to point out, it was better than nothing, and nicely paid for the vacation at the inn with some left over. Both of them left Lookaway Mountain. Both kissed Lexi lightly on the cheek, saying they hoped they hadn't inconvenienced her. And both sincerely vowed never to get involved in questionable schemes ever again.

Frank and Keith had gone with the government agents to Greensboro to report success.

Lexi was faced with a decision. Would she take the job of hostess at the inn now that Bob was out of it, or would she wait and wonder and dream of Keith and hope for a future with him? The more she thought of the hostess job, the more she wondered if she had the patience to deal with it. Finally, it was not difficult to decide that if her hope for Keith's love turned to ashes, she'd give the job serious consideration, but Keith came first.

Lexi had moved back to her apartment and was working in the back room of her gallery when the usual ring of the doorbell alerted her. With her heart fluttering, she entered the gallery.

Keith had come back.

For a long moment they stood looking at each other. Then he drew her into his arms, tightening them around her as they kissed. Lexi's senses were intoxicated.

"Magic," Keith whispered. "You are pure magic, darling. I love you so much and want you for my own."

"Do you mean—"

"I mean I want you to be my wife. For now and forever, my love."